Tiny Tales

Yorkshire & Lincolnshire

First published in Great Britain in 2007 by
Young Writers, Remus House, Coltsfoot Drive,
Peterborough, PE2 9JX
Tel (01733) 890066 Fax (01733) 313524
All Rights Reserved

© Copyright Contributors 2007
SB ISBN 978-1-84431-308-2

Disclaimer
Young Writers has maintained every effort
to publish stories that will not cause offence.
Any stories, events or activities relating to individuals
should be read as fictional pieces and not construed
as real-life character portrayal.

Foreword

Young Writers was established in 1991, with the aim of encouraging the children and young adults of today to think and write creatively. Our latest primary school competition, *Tiny Tales*, posed an exciting challenge for these young authors: to write, in no more than fifty words, a story encompassing a beginning, a middle and an end. We call this the mini saga.

Tiny Tales Yorkshire & Lincolnshire is our latest offering from the wealth of young talent that has mastered this incredibly challenging form. With such an abundance of imagination, humour and ability evident in such a wide variety of stories, these young writers cannot fail to enthral and excite with every tale.

Contents

Arkengarthdale CE Primary School, Richmond

James Stones (10) 13
Jacob Taylor-Neale (11) 14
Ella Stokes (8) 15
Aislinn Smith (11) 16
Thomas Markham (9) 17
Kelsie Hendry (9) 18
Louise Stones (9) 19
Kate Hodgson (9)..20
Megan Lundberg (7) 21
Samya Kelly (10) 22
Hannah Coates (11)......................................23
Thomas Coates (9) 24
Olivia Stones (8)..25

Birchwood Junior School, Birchwood

Thomas Pugh (11)...26
Rebecca Logan (9) 27
Lewis Ware (10)...28
Misha Chapman (11) 29
Sophie Pilbeam (11)......................................30
Lynsey Macer (11)...31
Connor Fewster (10)......................................32
Alex Stenner (10)...33
Daniel Fleming (10) 34

John Sleaford (11)&
Robert Wilkinson (10) 35
Brandon Greenhough (10) 36
Macauley Dunkin (10) 37
Joel Aldridge (10) 38
Kyle Bourke (9)..39
Callum Mulhall (10) 40
Chloe Bowness (10) 41
Hollie Wall (10) 42
Kieran Edghill (10)..43
Sophie Gottschall (11) 44
Daisy Wakefield (11) 45
Jessica Davison (11), Jordan Rudd,
Alan Cuthbert, Jadannah Holehouse (10),
Jamie Shipmans & Adam Crook (9) 46
Sophie Brown (10)...47
Joshua Healey (11) 48
Ethan Tonks (10)..49
Amy Brunton (9) 50
Lauren Capon (10) 51
Milli Lane-Taylor (11).......................................52
Rebecca Hall (10) 53
Porcher Tounbee (10)....................................54
Megan Barnsdale (9) 55
James Vickers (10)...56
Jacob Kerr (11)..57

Cononley CP School, Keighley

Martha Radley (11) 58
Joel Birks (11) 59
Niki Chatburn (11) 60
Rebecca Howard (11) 61
Chloe Aldham (11) 62
Catherine Hosker (11) 63

Ecclesfield Primary School, Ecclesfield

Grace Marshall (11) 64
Bradley Smith (11) 65
Georgia Else (10) 66
Thomas Solway (11) 67
Joshua Green (11) 68
Shauna Briggs (11) 69
Sophie Ellson (10) 70
Jessica Weston (11) 71
Samuel Brameld (10) 72
Michael Bettinson (11) 73
Courtney Williamson (11) 74
Jamie Raynor (10) 75
Molly Crookes (11) 76
Lewis Hurdley (11) 77
Alix Ward (11) 78
Hollie Ladyman (11) 79
Lucy Hufton (11) 80

Grassington CE Primary School, Skipton

Oscar Nutter (9) 81
James Alderson Edwards (8) 82
Emily Hobbs (8) 83
Harry Binns (8) 84
Lucy Fattorini (9) 85
Bethan Thomas (8) 86
James Darwin (8) 87
Anna Chrich (7) 88
Marty Fraser-Turner (9) 89
Saffy Mcleish (8) 90
Kate Tulley (9) 91
Jenni-Kate Moore (8) 92
Danielle Simpson (9) 93
Henry Hibbs (7) 94
Lydia Shepherd (9) 95

Headlands Primary School, Haxby

Emily Knowles (11) 96
Alex Lee (11) 97
Alexandra Haigh (11) 98
Jack Harrison (11) 99
Ryan Barker (10) 100
Megan Varley (10) 101
Sam Pratt (9) 102
Daniel McClusky (10) 103
Clementine Hyde (9) 104
Ellie Higginbotham (9) 105
Joel Lishman (10) 106
Catherine Nicholson (10) 107
William Peck (10) 108
Ellen Dawson (10) 109
Bethany Ellis (11) 110

Callum Mackenzie (10) 111
Ryan Kenealy (11) 112
Lily Campbell (9) 113
Ella Warren (10) 114
Phoebe Clarke (10) 115
Emily Beal (9) 116
Georgia Padfield (11) 117
Olivia Haigh (6) 118
Ellie Sutherland (7) 119
Alexandra Richardson (9) 120
Lauren Elizabeth Garnett (6) 121
Luke Dickinson (7) 122
Simran Atwal (7) 123
Lewis Frank (10) 124
Katie Sutton (8) 125
Billy Warren (8) 126
Thomas Reed (9) 127
Alexandra Copley (8) 128
Katrina Hopkins (10) 129

Leadenham CE Primary School, Lincoln

Abigail Everett (9) 130
James Delaney (9) 131
Ben Mott (8) 132
Charlie Cade (8) 133
Kelsey MacBain (9) 134
Eleanor Hall (9) 135
Luca Simeoli-Brown (9) 136
Jessica Everett (11) 137
Matty Williams (11) 138

Rhianna Jackson (10) 139
Emily Mott (9) 140
Henry Newton (11) 141
Wilf Chapman-Gandy (9) 142
Rebecca Holland (9) 143

Maltby Redwood J&I School, Rotherham

Lee Trigg (11) 144
Oliver Smith (11) 145
Oliver Connolly (11) 146
Thomas Westwood (11) 147
Lyle Copley (11) 148
Laura Martin (11) 149
Samuel Shore (11) 150
Ewan Brown (11) 151
Charlotte Hosier (11) 152
Beth Anderson (11) 153
Kathryn Essex (11) 154
Eleanor Hill (10) 155
Mitchell Parker (11) 156
Karen Glaves (11) 157
Thomas Shore (11) 158

Methodist J&I School, Wakefield

Courtney Bowen (11) 159
William Hirst (11) 160
Beth Goldthorpe (11) 161
Matthew Stephenson (10) 162
Aidan Piper (10) 163
Charlotte Clarkson (11) 164

Rio Shaw (11) 165
Holly Holt (11) 166
Dale Clark, Melissa McDade & Catherine
Aylward (11) 167
Alex Luo (11) 168
Shannon Dickinson (11) 169
Jacob Earnshaw (10) 170
Max Holman (10) 171
Kimberley Dudley (11) 172
Elliott Armitage (11) 173

Micklefield CE Primary School, Leeds
Lewis Short (10) 174
John Bland (10) 175
Ashley Sylvester (11) 176
Emma Gledhill (10) 177
Jessica Melia (10) 178
Ryan White (11) 179
Libby Jones (10) 180
Charlotte Keeble (11) 181
Adam Saunders (10) 182
Georgia Hargrave (10) 183

Northstead CP School, Scarborough
Jacob Hird (10) 184
Katie Wallace 185
Rachel Head 186
Jordan Hookem 187
Esme Ripley 188
Isaac Wilsher 189

Joe Eaveson 190
Molly Sheader (10) 191
Zachary Slater 192
Ben Foster 193
Hayley Towell 194
Sam Hepples 195
Ella Whelan 196
Amy Potton 197

Otley All Saints CE Primary School, Leeds
Joshua Walker (11) 198
Hal Laverty (11) 199
Louis Cook (11) 200
Leo Hannan (11) 201
Afnan Ezzeldin (11) 202
Grace Pollard (11) 203
Sophie Elliott (10) 204
Tegan Senior (11) 205
Olivia White (11) 206
Oliver Proctor (11) 207
James Gardner (11) 208
Emma Tranter (11) 209

Rawmarsh Monkwood Junior School, Rawmarsh
Joe Scott (11) 210

St Andrew's CE Primary School, Leasingham
Samuel James 211

Jack Whalen (10) 212
Emily Robinson (11) 213
Keely McNiffe 214
Nathan Carne (11) 215
Danny Ward (11) 216
Robert Wiles (11) 217
Lauren Culpan (10) 218
Leah Hammatt (11) 219
Alex Dickinson 220
Charlene Cowap (11) 221
Chloë Banks (11) 222
Zak Smith (11) 223
Sam Boughton (11) 224
Megan Curnow (11) 225

St Andrews Junior School, Brighouse

Claire Saxby (7) 226
Annalie Pearson (8) 227
Liberty Hodgson (8) 228
Bradley Mason 229
Jamie Browne (8) 230
Bethany Knight (8) 231
Jack Barraclough (8) 232
Edward Priestley (8) 233
Jade Littlewood (8) 234
Charlotte Hopley (8) 235
Damian Wales (8) 236
Lochlan Graham (8) 237
Thomas Metcalfe 238
Holly Kitteringham (7) 239
Millie Clegg (8) 240

St Hilda's School, Wakefield

Zara Dunford (9) 241
Elizabeth Grimes (9) 242
Abigail Edson (9) 243
Isabel Kaye (9) 244
Amelia Wain (9) 245
Zoya Karim (9) 246
Kyrie McConnell (8) 247
Katie Crowther (8) 248
Annabelle Brook (7) 249
Tilly Nicholls (8) 250
Charlotte Oldroyd (8) 251
Jennifer Watson (8) 252
Victoria Newton (8) 253
Paris Mann (8) 254
Maria Brook (7) 255
Olivia Stead (8) 256
Meera Sharma (8) 257
Helena Watford (8) 258

St Mary's Catholic Primary School, Knaresborough

Sine Kelly (10) 259
Francesca Recchia (10) 260
Alexander Ashton-Evans (10) 261
Lucy Noctor (9) 262
Rebecca Stockman (10) 263
Jordan Firth (10) 264
Alice Bryant (10) 265
Libby Owens (10) 266
Sabrina Gaertner (10) 267

Charlie Baker (10) 268
Jordan Tear (10) 269
Danielle Huggon (10) 270
Jacob Fincham-Dukes (10).....................271

St Mary's RC Primary School, Boston
Kerrie Turner (8) 272
Emma Thornalley (9) 273
Niall Larkin (9) 274
Rio Upsall (8)..275
Justyna Dombek (9)................................276

Shelf J&I School, Halifax
Lucy Nove (9) 277
Chester Robinson (11) 278
Cassie Lewis (11)....................................279
Jessica Foulds (11) 280
Rhys Wardman (11) 281
Megan Lee (8) 282
Brodie Wilson (11) 283
Bradley Power (10) 284
Dominic Prentice (11)...............................285
Elliott Parkinson (11).................................286
Sebastian Megson (11) 287
Ashley Stewart (11) 288
Sophie Leek (11) 289
Hannah Poulter (11) 290
Matthew Crabtree (11) 291
Daniel Marsden (11).................................292
Joseph Lumb (10) 293
Daniel Wilson (11) 294

Sowerby CP School, Thirsk
Emily Stott (10) 295
Jack McLauchlan (10)..............................296
Gemma Reynard (10)...............................297
Amy Booth (11) 298
Laura Cook (9) 299
Callum Stewart (9)...................................300
Rebecca Walker (11)................................301

The Mini Sagas

Tiny Tales Yorkshire & Lincolnshire

What Will Happen?

Here I am, all my friends are watching as I look at the section. What is going to happen? I watch a rider. He doesn't make it. I must make it. As I mount my trial bike and ride up all the steps. No problem!

James Stones (10)
Arkengarthdale CE Primary School, Richmond

The Tunnel

In a crazy world there lived unimaginable things. Noises like tigers and elephants and wacky gun sounds.
I took my first step, five minutes later I found myself on the other side of the tunnel, confronted with the best fair in the world. It turned out to be great.

Jacob Taylor-Neale (11)
Arkengarthdale CE Primary School, Richmond

Shine

This was it, the time had come. I stared in the mirror at myself. This was my opportunity to shine, I'd show them how to do it properly. I was still as a statue. I walked into the dark. A light shone on me, I curtsied and then I danced.

Ella Stokes (8)
Arkengarthdale CE Primary School, Richmond

The Mystery

The mystery was heaved out of its home, it was so much bigger than the previous one.
She started to tell me about the mystery.
We started off slow then we went faster. I enjoyed my mystery ride.
It came to the end. I dismounted Bonnie, the mystery; my horse.

Aislinn Smith (11)
Arkengarthdale CE Primary School, Richmond

It

I was shaking with fear because I heard a rustling in the trees. A shadow passed over me, I heard a scream. It was my brother, he was gone. Then I heard it.
'Thomas, Thomas, Thomas!' then I saw it; ten eyes, green slime, gross! Then *poof!* I woke up.

Thomas Markham (9)
Arkengarthdale CE Primary School, Richmond

Flies

Dad's boss came for dinner. First course; tomato soup with bread, my favourite. I'll make Dad crack. I got a roll, I dipped it in my soup, I held it over my face, I dropped it, it plopped in my mouth. I got the fly swatter and licked it. Gross.

Kelsie Hendry (9)
Arkengarthdale CE Primary School, Richmond

Winning

My heart was thudding. What was going to happen? My pony was still as a brick. I was doing saddle-up and go. Then I had to move to the corner, then another person stood next to me, then another and another. Then my name was called. I had won.

Louise Stones (9)
Arkengarthdale CE Primary School, Richmond

Cuddles

I was worried, my heart thudded. Was I going to do it or was I going to fall off? I thundered towards the jump, I went over but I lay on the ground.
I laid on my bed thinking how well I'd done at getting over the jump on Cuddles.

Kate Hodgson (9)
Arkengarthdale CE Primary School, Richmond

The Hideous Scary Thing

I was just putting my pyjamas on in the hotel room that we were staying in when suddenly the door squeaked open. A hideous scary thing slowly started to walk closer and closer. Suddenly I saw who it was, it was Gran in her hideous big see-through nightie.

Megan Lundberg (7)
Arkengarthdale CE Primary School, Richmond

Find The Clues

I looked around. I could trust no one. I looked down at the clues in my hand. They all pointed to one thing. In came my suspects. I couldn't be wrong! My suspicions confirmed, I made my accusations. 'Mrs Peacock, the spanner, the library.'
I always take Cluedo too seriously!

Samya Kelly (10)
Arkengarthdale CE Primary School, Richmond

Murderers At The Dining Table

Goosepimples emerging down my spine, my heart beating faster than an Olympic runner, sweat flowing down my forehead like the Nile. The murderer is expecting me to eat the poison. Dad has already fallen for it and soon will be gone. But nothing will make me eat Brussels sprouts.

Hannah Coates (11)
Arkengarthdale CE Primary School, Richmond

Spoon Of Doom

Here it comes, the spoon of doom. The spoon that had nothing anyone had ever tasted. The spoon that made you the size of a golf ball. The spoon was shoved in my mouth, all I could taste was peas mixed with Brussels sprouts, the things I hate the most.

Thomas Coates (9)
Arkengarthdale CE Primary School, Richmond

Tiny Tales Yorkshire & Lincolnshire

Baa Baa Black Sheep

Hi I'm a sheep called Baa Baa Black Sheep. I know what you are going to ask me, have I any wool?
I need a haircut this minute and so filled the bags full. Now how many bags full did you need? Three? The farmer took them home happily.

Olivia Stones (8)
Arkengarthdale CE Primary School, Richmond

Shocked!

One evening there was a knock on the door, when I went to answer it, I stopped. What if it was a person with a gun? So I ignored it and went to bed.
The next day I realised that it was a £10,000 cheque from the lottery. Oh no!

Thomas Pugh (11)
Birchwood Junior School, Birchwood

Horror House

I slowly walked up to the haunted house.
'Look out, here comes the vampire!' someone screamed.
There he was. I froze in terror. Tall and thin, wearing a black cape, walking towards me. I stared as he took off his mask.
It was my dad on Hallowe'en.

Rebecca Logan (9)
Birchwood Junior School, Birchwood

Aliens In The Night

There I was in bed. Suddenly there was a flash of light. I looked out the window, aliens were walking to my house. I panicked, I jumped into bed. There was knocking on the door. I walked downstairs, I opened the door then I remembered it was Hallowe'en.

Lewis Ware (10)
Birchwood Junior School, Birchwood

Tiny Tales Yorkshire & Lincolnshire

Alien Landing

I sat there stiffly, watching in fear, doing nothing at all. The lasers firing, guns shooting, worst of all, *people dying!* Blood everywhere and my best friend Megan sobbing her heart out. 'Argh help!' Why, why me? Why did I have to choose this rotten film?

Misha Chapman (11)
Birchwood Junior School, Birchwood

Gone For Good

The plane flew over the woods, people flying to their destination. *All of a sudden* ... the engine failed, lights flickered. Screams non-stop! Then ... silence, the plane had crashed.
People rushed to the disaster, but all they found were skid marks and paper. The plane and people *gone forever!*

Sophie Pilbeam (11)
Birchwood Junior School, Birchwood

The Monster

As it grew dark I climbed into bed, checking under my bed and in my wardrobe. Something scratched at my door. The monster! I buried my head in my pillow and my heart pounded. The door slowly creaked open.
Phew! the monster was just Jessie, my cat.

Lynsey Macer (11)
Birchwood Junior School, Birchwood

The Secret Birthday Party

It was Saturday morning, that meant it was Jack's birthday. His mum and dad had planned a secret birthday.
He went off to football training …
1 hour later he came back. 'Surprise!' everyone shouted and he had a good day.

Connor Fewster (10)
Birchwood Junior School, Birchwood

The Disastrous Spell

Let me think what I will put in … A dead rat, a litre of mud, some frogs' legs, an eyeball and a tarantula. Oh no, it's fizzing up madly. I will put in some teeth. 'Argh!' *Bang!* Phew! Only a daydream.

Alex Stenner (10)
Birchwood Junior School, Birchwood

Untitled

There I was, sitting in my driver's seat, happily singing along to The Fray. I had seven passengers on board. Suddenly someone shot the door off. I put the train on auto and ran to catch them but it was only a hungry passenger trying to eat a door.

Daniel Fleming (10)
Birchwood Junior School, Birchwood

Sacrificial

When Sarah took her dog for a walk one day she found an ancient sacrificial ground. She went closer and she found a scroll. It said: 'You cannot leave until you shout, take me!' So she shouted, 'Take me!' and something grabbed her, it was her brother playing a trick.

**John Sleaford (11)
& Robert Wilkinson (10)**
Birchwood Junior School, Birchwood

They Have Landed

People ran through the dull streets, there were vast explosions. 'Argh!' the citizens screamed as strange shadows hovered overhead. My hands began to tremble and legs began to shake. As the metal titan landed, breathing acid fumes everyone ran towards the beasts. A hatch opened and the aliens had landed …

Brandon Greenhough (10)
Birchwood Junior School, Birchwood

Aliens

When James was going through the dark, creepy park he met a slimy alien. *How?* he thought. *It can't be.*
The alien mumbled, 'I will eat you!'
James shrieked, 'Help!'
Bob ran in the way of the alien to find out. It was James' bizarre mum dressed as an alien!

Macauley Dunkin (10)
Birchwood Junior School, Birchwood

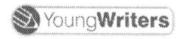

When Hyper Rhinos Attack

One day, all was normal. Then, hyper space rhinos came in shiny silver crafts, blowing up the world. One bomb hit me. I screamed and closed my eyes. Then, I opened them and I saw ordinary zoo rhinos. I never liked them again.

Joel Aldridge (10)
Birchwood Junior School, Birchwood

The Bizarre Experiment

In a dark laboratory scientists were thinking of a solution, how to create a living monster. Suddenly one of the scientists dropped the solution and it spread into another solution. It began to turn into a greeny colour. It made a monster. The two scientists fainted.

Kyle Bourke (9)
Birchwood Junior School, Birchwood

Scary School

As Callum started to walk down the corridor after school he heard a *roar!* The boy started running. It got louder. *Roar!* Then he saw the scariest dinosaur, it had a baby dinosaur. Callum was terrified but then he realised it was his 2 friends and their dog.

Callum Mulhall (10)
Birchwood Junior School, Birchwood

It Went Wrong

My hands were shivering, the heat from the pan made me sweat. A sprinkle of salt, a dash of toad and a cupful of sweaty blood. *Bam! Crash! Woah!* Suddenly my sister was a blood-drenched toad. Argh! I think my spell might have gone wrong, badly wrong! Ha!

Chloe Bowness (10)
Birchwood Junior School, Birchwood

The Magic Spell That Went Wrong

I stood there making my spell. I wondered if it would all go wrong. I heard giggling in the magic pot. I was hoping I'd not gone wrong. I wondered if a ghost was inside the magic pot, then my sister popped out!

Hollie Wall (10)
Birchwood Junior School, Birchwood

The Game Of …

When I walked in the house I could hear voices and things getting hit. The lights were flickering on and off. I felt scared, I felt like a freezing cold knife was slicing through my back.
I walked in the hall.
Oh great, I love tennis.

Kieran Edghill (10)
Birchwood Junior School, Birchwood

The Mad Scientist

Long ago, in a small dark laboratory, there lived a lonesome, mad scientist. He was planning to create a monster so he could be famous. He carefully put in multicoloured potions one by one, putting in tiny droplets each time. Then, the table started shaking and … it just exploded.

Sophie Gottschall (11)
Birchwood Junior School, Birchwood

The Alienated Hamster

I woke up one morning to hear a very odd squeaking coming from my hamster's cage. I looked over and saw his eyes were glowing. 'Argh!' I screamed, 'What happened to you?' I asked, then … I realised … he had been alienated!

Daisy Wakefield (11)
Birchwood Junior School, Birchwood

Hot Ash

I could hear rumbling in the distance. People ran from their houses screaming. The smell of poisonous fumes filled my nose. Grey ash floated down from the sky. I started to feel scared, then it happened, like a sudden bolt of lightning. Lava came pouring from the erupting volcano.

Jessica Davison (11), Jordan Rudd, Alan Cuthbert, Jadannah Holehouse (10), Jamie Shipmans & Adam Crook (9)
Birchwood Junior School, Birchwood

Blue Grass And Green Rain?
The Day Nature Changed

Fifty years ago grass was not green but blue! This was until one day, it rained so much it dyed the grass green. When the rain evaporated it took the blue colouring too! So today we have green grass and blue rain.
Well until next raining season!

Sophie Brown (10)
Birchwood Junior School, Birchwood

Kane's Birthday

One day Kane went to school. He put his bag on his peg. Suddenly the classroom door creaked open. He peered next door but no one was there. Suddenly his classroom door creaked again. He walked into his classroom, then his class shouted, 'Happy birthday!'

Joshua Healey (11)
Birchwood Junior School, Birchwood

I Saw!

While I was hiding behind a rock I heard a roar. I stuck my head out from behind it, I saw … nothing but a tiny bird pecking for worms so I stood up and hid behind a tree. Unfortunately there was nothing. When I turned around slowly I saw dinosaurs!

Ethan Tonks (10)
Birchwood Junior School, Birchwood

Spell Gone Wrong

Here I go with my spell. I put the potions in and it started to bubble. I thought this was normal. I was waiting right next to the pot. All of a sudden it stopped bubbling. What is happening? Out jumped my teachers! 'Oh no,' I screamed!

Amy Brunton (9)
Birchwood Junior School, Birchwood

The Surprise Birthday

I went to school one day. I thought it was Saturday.
No one was there. The floor creaked. I felt all tense. I carried on asking myself, *what is that?* The door opened, squeaking then, *rahhhh!* I realised it was a surprise birthday party!

Lauren Capon (10)
Birchwood Junior School, Birchwood

Disaster In The Kitchen

I was making a cake for my granny's birthday party. It had chocolate in it and sugar on the top.
I heard the phone ring in the hallway, so I answered. Half an hour later I smelt something cooking from the kitchen, *fire!*

Milli Lane-Taylor (11)
Birchwood Junior School, Birchwood

The Magic Spell That Goes Wrong

'I am going to make a magic spell today,' said the scientist. He got all the stuff he needed together. The scientist had a huge pot and a huge spoon. He put in all the ingredients and … *boom!* The pot exploded like an erupting volcano.

Rebecca Hall (10)
Birchwood Junior School, Birchwood

The Rainbow Night

Blue, black and white was the colour of the shimmering night. I went to bed and out of my window I saw yellow and orange stars. It reached 12, midnight and blue came out, the yellow and orange stars went home. I said goodnight. They said goodnight.

Porcher Tounbee (10)
Birchwood Junior School, Birchwood

The Journey

The thrill of hopping into a car when the moon was gleaming got Maddison excited. The stars grew brighter as the night grew old. Shivers shot up Maddison's body, she wondered how the journey would end. Her head tilted and rose to see what was standing in front of her …

Megan Barnsdale (9)
Birchwood Junior School, Birchwood

Bang!

Crash!
'You little hooligan, that's my car!'
'I hate Bean.'
'Yeah so do I!'
'Let's get him!' screamed the angry people as they charged towards him.
'Argh!' shrieked Mr Bean as he ran towards his house. He jumped out of his window to get away and landed with a bang!

James Vickers (10)
Birchwood Junior School, Birchwood

The FFH (Fat Flying Horse)

Pegasus bounded over the thicket, or so he thought he did. He was now old and overweight, breathless, he struggled through the wood. He now came to a large canyon. He jumped and flapped his wings frantically, but he was too fat so he tumbled 100 feet to his death.

Jacob Kerr (11)
Birchwood Junior School, Birchwood

An Undiscovered Secret

An intrepid explorer travelled far and wide to discover … a secret. This secret was an island. It seemed pretty normal apart from a huge crater filled with thick mud in the centre. Suddenly the mud bubbled as he stepped on the land.

After hours the brave man got sucked in …

Martha Radley (11)
Cononley CP School, Keighley

A Deadly Mistake

Once scientists tried an experiment which went terribly wrong. They tried something just for fun but created an evil monster. Everybody in the town fled for their lives but not Steve. He fought the beast.

It roared, 'Steve, Steve!'

I awoke.

'Wake up Steve!' It was my English teacher.

Joel Birks (11)
Cononley CP School, Keighley

Magic Spell Goes Wrong

As I was in the filthy box, they covered me in a black cloth. The assistant said to me that there was a door at the back of the cupboard but there wasn't. He said, 'Expelliamus!' then opened the door. I wasn't there. I looked around, it was black ... 'Help!'

Niki Chatburn (11)
Cononley CP School, Keighley

Nightmare Begins

Here it comes … closer … 'No, no, no!' The beady eyes stared at me, I was scared, there was nothing I could do now. I was trapped … 'Help! Help! Please someone help.' I could hear the slithering of the snake getting closer whilst hissing. 'Go away, Mum, help me … help me!'

Rebecca Howard (11)
Cononley CP School, Keighley

Magician's Box

As I lay in total darkness … I heard the magician break the silence in the room.
'I will begin.'
The crowd were laughing, cheering (which made me panic)! All of a sudden I saw light. The magician smiled at me. I knew I was OK. I was safe and sound!

Chloe Aldham (11)
Cononley CP School, Keighley

A Wartime Tale

The German planes (as they had German flags on) were zooming overhead. I had to get away so I ran for my life. The planes were dropping bombs behind me. One catapulted me into the air ... the next thing I knew was that I was in hospital for life.

Catherine Hosker (11)
Cononley CP School, Keighley

Space

From here you can see the pebble-like planet spinning forever and ever. The blue twinkles in the sun like a sapphire with rocks of brown and green. From here I can see footprints, everlasting footprints positioned perfectly, leading up to the spaceship and marks in the moon dust.

Grace Marshall (11)
Ecclesfield Primary School, Ecclesfield

The Incredible Fear Of

...

The ground shook, my seat rocked, the rumbling pierced a hole in my ear. 'Argh! Get me down!'
We were cutting through the air. All of a sudden we were tossed and tipped, my heart in my mouth. Phew, back to normal, all that time I panicked.
'I'll fly again!'

Bradley Smith (11)
Ecclesfield Primary School, Ecclesfield

It

John went to play with his boat. The boat went in a drain.
'Is this what you're looking for?' said a clown.
John took the boat.
'Do you want a balloon?' John took his hand out and the clown dragged him in.
John was never seen ever again …

Georgia Else (10)
Ecclesfield Primary School, Ecclesfield

Hallowe'en

He was walking home from school when he saw a mysterious object in the corner. He got closer and saw it was a note. It said, 'Don't look behind you and don't blink!' He looked behind. There stood a man with a knife. 'Surprise! Happy Hallowe'en!' It was his friend.

Thomas Solway (11)
Ecclesfield Primary School, Ecclesfield

Accidental Spell

There was a very cute couple who came across an old magician. The old man bellowed, 'Hocus pocus.' In a blink of an eye they flew up into the sky and landed. But when they landed very, very softly they had switched bodies. In seconds they were in original bodies.

Joshua Green (11)
Ecclesfield Primary School, Ecclesfield

A Trip Down Memory Lane

I'm all by myself in a room of dark memories, slowing losing happiness and strength as I sail along my path of the past from Hell. From bad injuries to fatal. As I sit and drown in tears of time my friends sit around me in my coma, crying, heartbroken.

Shauna Briggs (11)
Ecclesfield Primary School, Ecclesfield

Untitled

It was pitch-black outside and there was also thunder and lightning. A girl called Nicole was laying in bed. She finally awoke and could hear a creaking sound, it was coming from the landing. As Nicole slowly got out of bed she realised it was all a dream.

Sophie Ellson (10)
Ecclesfield Primary School, Ecclesfield

The Spell

Crash! Bang! Boom! 'Nooo!' All of the lights went out. Josie couldn't see what she was doing in the kitchen.

'Maybe I shouldn't have mixed the fish food with the cola,' she said to herself. That was the perfect spell to get my brother back … his PlayStation!

Jessica Weston (11)
Ecclesfield Primary School, Ecclesfield

The Hungry Caterpillar

The little caterpillar was starving so he started eating a big leaf, munching and crunching until there was no more leaf left. Then he wrapped himself up in a sparkly silver cocoon.
In the morning the cocoon started to shake violently. Then suddenly, out popped the most beautiful butterfly.

Samuel Brameld (10)
Ecclesfield Primary School, Ecclesfield

Terrified

I'm engulfed in fog. At least I can rely on my compass. It spins wildly. I try to turn the plane but can't. I begin to panic. I'm pulled into the murky depths. I scream as the cockpit fills with water. It's above my neck. I begin to drown. Terrified.

Michael Bettinson (11)
Ecclesfield Primary School, Ecclesfield

Struggling Below

My head bobbed under and my lungs started to fill. I spluttered, trying to find the last bit of air, choking on the way. My whole body shook and trembled rapidly. Nearly losing consciousness firm hands hooked under my arms and pulled me to safety.

Thank goodness we have lifeguards.

Courtney Williamson (11)
Ecclesfield Primary School, Ecclesfield

Attack Of The Loch Ness Monster

I was down under, unable to breathe. The sea crushing me and my dignity. The Loch Ness monster was real. It was biting my leg. The pain, it was killing me. I held on to the monster for a bit. By this time I was dead, never to be seen again.

Jamie Raynor (10)
Ecclesfield Primary School, Ecclesfield

The Beast

Sara looked around but there was nobody in sight. She started climbing out of the pool, when she spotted a large beast in the distance. A large shiver went speeding down her spine. Suddenly the beast span around and turned into a human and started watering some plants.

Molly Crookes (11)
Ecclesfield Primary School, Ecclesfield

Time Trapped

'It's ready!'
'Are you sure?'
'Positive!'
Tom's excitement took over, throwing him into the cockpit.
'What're you doing?'
'Testing it!'
He pulled in the professor, then pressed the time travel button. A bright light blinded them, then faded, showing WWII Britain. A bullet slammed into the engine. *Boom!*

Lewis Hurdley (11)
Ecclesfield Primary School, Ecclesfield

Three Little Pigs

The three little pigs used three different materials to build three different houses. A wolf appeared and blew two of the three houses down. The wolf tried to blow the last house down so he jumped into the chimney, *argh!* The wolf had burnt his bum.

Alix Ward (11)
Ecclesfield Primary School, Ecclesfield

Aliens Land In My Garden

There was a strange whirring sound coming from the back garden. I went outside and there, right in front of me was a huge spaceship. I knew at that moment that today, for the first ever time, aliens had landed on Earth.

Hollie Ladyman (11)
Ecclesfield Primary School, Ecclesfield

The Hopeless Witch

The witch cast a spell on a frog. 'You're going to be a human,' said the witch in a gloomy voice. With a sudden bang the frog turned into a hopeless sheep, then with another sudden bang the sheep disappeared, 'Oh well,' said the witch.

Lucy Hufton (11)
Ecclesfield Primary School, Ecclesfield

Tiny Tales Yorkshire & Lincolnshire

The Search For The Little Boy

A boy lived by the woods. He went for a walk in the field. He was ambushed by a wolf. The wolf kidnapped the boy.
A search party started. The boy's mother found his soft coat outside a cave. They killed the wolf and the boy kept his cosy coat.

Oscar Nutter (9)
Grassington CE Primary School, Skipton

Creature Trap

Yesterday Tom was walking down the street with his mum, dad, sister and his baby brother and sister.
Bang! Crash! Bang! An immense ship came down. 'Wow!' said Tom. Then the police came heavy-handed.
The ship fell to the Earth then heavy trucks came to take it all away.

James Alderson Edwards (8)
Grassington CE Primary School, Skipton

The Annoying Brother

When Rachel got home she saw a trail of blood leading to the kitchen. She followed it.
'Fooled you!' yelled her brother.
'Stop it,' sighed Rachel. But when she went to bed she screamed because a monster jumped out at her!
'Fooled you!' Brother laughed.
Then Rachel started laughing too.

Emily Hobbs (8)
Grassington CE Primary School, Skipton

The Loch Ness Monster

One day I went to Scotland to find the Loch Ness monster. My mum happily took me to Scotland. When I got there I went straight to find the Loch Ness monster. I couldn't see it. A second later I glimpsed its tail.

Harry Binns (8)
Grassington CE Primary School, Skipton

Holly Dreamy Day

Once there was a girl called Holly. One day her mind went blank. There was a monster she thought was in a cupboard. She assumed it had taken her mind away and put it in drawers. She looked and looked …
'Holly! Stop daydreaming!' screamed her teacher.

Lucy Fattorini (9)
Grassington CE Primary School, Skipton

The Journey

My seat belt clicked as we started to move. My tummy was churning. I opened the window. I felt my tummy lunging. I opened the window more. We drove to the service station. I got to the toilet in time but I threw up.
I'm travel sick. I hate it!

Bethan Thomas (8)
Grassington CE Primary School, Skipton

Alien World

Tom had to go to bed when a bang went off. In Tom's garden was a huge spaceship. A little door opened and there was a monster. It climbed through the window. Then he came upstairs and opened the big door. Tom shouted, 'Alien!' as he closed his eyes …

James Darwin (8)
Grassington CE Primary School, Skipton

The Shark

My fingers were trembling. I was too busy thinking about the shark. I was too scared. It got closer. I heard its teeth clashing as it ate another fish. I threw sand at it. It saw me. *Clash!* 'Ow!' It was only my sister pinching me.

Anna Chrich (7)
Grassington CE Primary School, Skipton

Doctor Who And Noo-Noo From Teletubbies

5 centuries ago Doctor Who travelled with Noo-Noo but never landed. 'I'm getting bored,' said Doctor but as soon as he finished, *boom!* They didn't land but Doctor looked out and Gandalf and Tinky-Winky were invading. 'Argh!' shouted Noo-Noo but he sucked them up.
'Well done Moouo,' praised Noo-Noo.

Marty Fraser-Turner (9)
Grassington CE Primary School, Skipton

The Scary Thing

During the evening Becky went to the deep, dark woods to collect firewood.
'What was that?' She took a step backwards and bumped into a tall, hairy, furry thing. He turned around and screamed like mad and went running home. She never found out what it was.

Saffy Mcleish (8)
Grassington CE Primary School, Skipton

Witch's Room

Once upon a time a little child named Sophie was playing in the garden when *wham!* she had gone.
She was in a room. She woke up to a bang on the head. She stood up and walked to a black cauldron, she reached in. *Bam!* She was back at home.

Kate Tulley (9)
Grassington CE Primary School, Skipton

Doctor, Rose And Martha In Space

Doctor and Martha found a rocket. A whole load of smoke suddenly came out. Then Rose came out. They looked at the controls. Suddenly it took off. Then hit the ground, then sand, then sea. Just in time they swam up and got to shore. *Boom!* It exploded.

Jenni-Kate Moore (8)
Grassington CE Primary School, Skipton

Untitled

One day two people were blasted into space. As soon as they got there aliens surrounded them. The woman tried to get something out of her pocket to scare the aliens away but instead a magnet fell out of her pocket and the aliens vanished.

Danielle Simpson (9)
Grassington CE Primary School, Skipton

Tom And Jerry

Tom was asleep. I walked around him. I climbed up the blind, opened the fridge and stole all of the food from the fridge. I chucked it in my mouse hole. Then I jumped off the fridge. Tom woke up and I ran to my hole. There I ate.

Henry Hibbs (7)
Grassington CE Primary School, Skipton

The Messy Alien

The alien landed, *splat!* in his dinner. The messy alien wiggled and giggled. *Splat!* again but in my face. I was not impressed.
'Goo-goo, messy, messy brother.'
'Mum,' I shouted. 'Milly has got me messy.'
'Bad girl, Milly. No, no don't do that, time to clean up, silly baby!'

Lydia Shepherd (9)
Grassington CE Primary School, Skipton

Cabbage Leaves

Suddenly Megan panicked, her rabbit's cage was wide open. Frantically rushing outside, she couldn't find Maisie anywhere. Searching, calling, no rabbit appeared. One last plan to try, Maisie's favourite fresh cabbage leaves. After patiently waiting, eventually, from her secret burrow, out hopped Maisie. Panic over!

Emily Knowles (11)
Headlands Primary School, Haxby

Racing Games

Come on, faster, faster. Hit the nitrous button. Come on, overtake that car. Just a bit further. Come on, skid round that corner, then just speed forward. Come on. Oohhh! Game over! So this means we don't get the prize of a PS3. Oh well, easy come, easy go.

Alex Lee (11)
Headlands Primary School, Haxby

The Billing Lake

As we drove into the lake, the water lapped over the bonnet and seeped in through the doors. I didn't expect it to be so deep but to my amazement we made it out the other side. I wish I had my dad's confidence in his Land Rover.

Alexandra Haigh (11)
Headlands Primary School, Haxby

Creepy House

There was a spooky deserted house. Ivy poured out of the cracks in the pale musty brick. A statue guarded the house with its gazing and cold stare. Huge iron gates creaked with rusty paint peeling off. The rotting wooden doors appeared towering over you. But did anyone live there?

Jack Harrison (11)
Headlands Primary School, Haxby

Dragon Slayer

Edward was a soldier who was sent by the king to retrieve gold from a dragon's lair.
He went through treacherous lands to find the lair and when he found it, he battled the dragon and slayed it!
He returned the gold and the king knighted him for his bravery.

Ryan Barker (10)
Headlands Primary School, Haxby

The Big Mistake

Mr Smith laid awake, dreading the week ahead. Mrs Smith was asleep. Why oh why had he agreed to this week off work? Oddly, he didn't want it.
This was it; he was alone in the house with the kids. Two heads peered round the door, it was half-term!

Megan Varley (10)
Headlands Primary School, Haxby

A Soul Of Many

I ran. I was in the graveyard, running. I was scared. I didn't look back. The moon flashing in the black sky. All I wanted was to get home. Suddenly I was grabbed. I was forced into a grave. I couldn't get out. I was dragged deeper and deeper … 'Argh!'

Sam Pratt (9)
Headlands Primary School, Haxby

Where Was He?

I brandished my blood-covered, scarlet-red sword. Trudging through a swamp of dead bodies, I saw him, he was the man that had killed my brother.
A sudden silence fell and was broken by us hurtling towards each other.
I later awoke, however, couldn't see anyone. Where was he?

Daniel McClusky (10)
Headlands Primary School, Haxby

The War At Night

The bombs were dropping fast. I was really scared. I could see the shadowy aeroplanes in the air. I could hear the terrifying buzzing sound. I closed my eyes and imagined it was the end. My heart was pounding like a drum in my chest. I ran, too late. Argh!

Clementine Hyde (9)
Headlands Primary School, Haxby

The Grand Race

No one thinks I'll make it. The finish line is just one lap away, but I'm coming sixth. Wait! There's a huge mudslide coming up and a banana skin! People are slipping all over the place in their cars! Now I'm in first place! Mario Kart is the best!

Ellie Higginbotham (9)
Headlands Primary School, Haxby

Holiday Time

The buzzing was getting louder. Suddenly all lights flickered moodily on. I could just make out a dark figure trudging towards me. A suitcase flew through the door!
'Joel, Joel.'
It carried on. 'Have you forgotten when our aeroplane takes off because it's time to go on holiday?' smiled Dad.

Joel Lishman (10)
Headlands Primary School, Haxby

The Super Caterpillar

'Help! I'm stuck in a flower!' said Mr Bee. Suddenly Super Caterpillar arrived and saved the bee by pulling really hard. But that wasn't it, someone else was in trouble. He saw an ant stuck pulling a leaf, so he went to help him and saved the tiny ant.

Catherine Nicholson (10)
Headlands Primary School, Haxby

Tom And The Dragon

There once was a fire-breathing dragon. Knights tried to defeat the dragon, they were unsuccessful.

Tom was brave and loved to fight. He decided to kill the dragon to become famous.

The door creaked as it opened. Nervously he attacked the dragon and fought well.

He was the champion!

William Peck (10)
Headlands Primary School, Haxby

Birthday Cake Problem

Splat! The birthday cake had slipped off the table and was now lying on the floor. His mum would kill him! All he had to do was go out and buy another one exactly the same.
He heard a car pull up on the drive. He was already too late.

Ellen Dawson (10)
Headlands Primary School, Haxby

Girl Power!

Once there was a girl, but she wasn't an ordinary girl, she had girl power. Everywhere she went and everything she did she would always need to use it.

One day she got a lucky charm which was just as good. The charm ran out. So did the power …

Bethany Ellis (11)
Headlands Primary School, Haxby

Jeff's Day

One day Jeff woke up. He got up and sprinted down the stairs. He scoffed his breakfast and ran to work as fast as his legs could take him. He got to work and because he was late he got fired.

He never got a job again!

Callum Mackenzie (10)
Headlands Primary School, Haxby

Nick And His Mum

When Nick and his mum were in the Anderson shelter they could hear the bombs going off in the distance.

In the morning Nick saw his dad with a bandage on his head walking towards him. His dad told him that he had come back because the war had ended.

Ryan Kenealy (11)
Headlands Primary School, Haxby

The Roller Coaster

My heart was thumping inside my chest. I was terrified because I wasn't sure what was going to happen next. I wished it would all stop. Just when I thought I was going to let out a yell the roller coaster came to a halt and I sighed with relief.

Lily Campbell (9)
Headlands Primary School, Haxby

The Bang From Downstairs

Crash! Rattle! Bang! 'What was that?' Fred crept downstairs whilst breathing heavily. He heard tiptoes coming towards him! All of a sudden a masked figure jumped out consequently making Fred scream. The masked person dashed to the door and yanked it open. Oh no! He'd got away! Fred was scared.

Ella Warren (10)
Headlands Primary School, Haxby

The Scarecrow That Came Upstairs

I screamed! The window creaked. I looked outside, what was it? A gloomy man walked towards my house. I shivered … the figure became clearer. I glared at a field nearby. It was gone! I panicked … This must be a dream, I blinked, I screamed! The scarecrow was … in my room!

Phoebe Clarke (10)
Headlands Primary School, Haxby

Birthday Surprise

Mum shouted up to me, 'Come on, Emily, we're going somewhere special.'
As we pulled up at the pet store my eyes widened with excitement!
We walked in and there was my dream rabbit which I called Digger. We're now living together.

Emily Beal (9)
Headlands Primary School, Haxby

Little Bo Peep

Josey bought dolls every day. However, this one was like no other. It was called … *Bo Peep.* That night Josey was in bed, Bo in the cupboard. 'Josey, I'm out the cupboard. Josey, I'm on the floor. Josey, I'm on the bed. Josey I'm behind you with a knife … *dead!'*

Georgia Padfield (11)
Headlands Primary School, Haxby

My Dog Ruby

Ruby Dog, she is my friend. She likes me and I play with her at the weekend. At night-time I go downstairs to see my dog and give her a bedtime hug and then I go back upstairs to my bed and go to sleep.

Olivia Haigh (6)
Headlands Primary School, Haxby

A Snowy Night

It was a snowy night and everyone was fast asleep in bed except James. He was climbing high up a hill when all of a sudden he slipped.

'Argh!'

'Wake up, James, you've fallen out of bed,' said his mum.

James climbed back into bed and fell fast asleep again!

Ellie Sutherland (7)
Headlands Primary School, Haxby

Fancy That!

Sophie invited me to her party. We discussed clothes, she mentioned a fancy dress. Mum and I made a chicken costume. Stepping into the party thirty pairs of eyes stared at me. Why oh why was Sophie wearing a sequinned dress? Oh no! she meant that kind of fancy dress!

Alexandra Richardson (9)
Headlands Primary School, Haxby

The Surprise

John opened the door and ran down the stairs. He didn't eat all his breakfast. He got into the car to go to his grandma's. But what would he say to his grandma?
When he arrived he had a card in his hand. It said 'Happy birthday Grandma'.

Lauren Elizabeth Garnett (6)
Headlands Primary School, Haxby

Ben's Dream

One night Ben was coming home from school when he saw a red glow in the sky. 'I wonder what that glow is?'
At that moment the red glow became even bigger, then he saw it was a UFO. When he looked again he was lying in his bed!

Luke Dickinson (7)
Headlands Primary School, Haxby

The Scary Wood

Once there was a girl called Kate. She was very bossy. She was walking through the wood. Suddenly she saw a ghost. The ghost ran after Kate. Kate ran as fast as she could but the ghost killed her. She was never ever, ever, ever, ever, ever, ever seen again.

Simran Atwal (7)
Headlands Primary School, Haxby

The Future

It was the year 3001 and everything was different. Us humans didn't work, robots called Roboton did. Until last week, that is. The robots changed and started a war, it was an amazing battle. Of course we won but I am the last human, when I die it's over.

Lewis Frank (10)
Headlands Primary School, Haxby

The Haunted House

I knocked on the door, no one answered. The lights were on. Then I heard a noise coming from inside. I put my hand on the handle. Suddenly it opened, I walked in. I heard the noise again. I rushed upstairs to see what it was. It was too late!

Katie Sutton (8)
Headlands Primary School, Haxby

The Bowl With A Letter In

He rushed downstairs, looked round, everything was gone. He went in the kitchen. He saw nothing but a bowl with a letter in. His eyes beamed at the bowl.
The door shut. *Bang!* He slowly walked towards the bowl and picked it up. He looked and it said

...

Billy Warren (8)
Headlands Primary School, Haxby

No Escape From The Enemy

The scorching burn of the leather whip felt fatal. I couldn't bear it much longer. I looked for an exit. The boulder was impossible to move, but there was light. I had a brilliant idea. I climbed up the boulder and got out, then an arrow landed in my chest.

Thomas Reed (9)
Headlands Primary School, Haxby

A Wet Adventure

The sea was lovely. Then I saw a fin coming towards me. My heart was beating fast, the fin started circling me. I tried to grab it. I missed, my legs were tired. I tried to hold the fin again.
I did it!
I loved swimming with Alexia the dolphin.

Alexandra Copley (8)
Headlands Primary School, Haxby

Emily Crept Up On Me!

As I walked something touched my back. I was scared. Just then I stopped and dropped my sweets. Then, I started to run as fast as a cat. My hands tingled like a light bulb switching on. Everything began to look blurry so I ran very fast back home.

Katrina Hopkins (10)
Headlands Primary School, Haxby

Nessy

As Nessy fiercely went scrounging for another glistening and divinely luxurious salmon, when suddenly … *splash!* A beautifully carved wooden crate floated gracefully to the bottom of Loch Ness. The crate beamed an enchanted light and whispered, 'I shall grant you two wishes.'
'I wish for friendship and to be loved.'

Abigail Everett (9)
Leadenham CE Primary School, Lincoln

Harry Potter And The Apparition Test

Harry Potter was at the ministry when … 'The test room is up ahead,' shouted Mr Weasley. Ahead there was a door saying 'Ministry of Magic Apparition Test Room'.
'Harry Potter,' said a stern voice. It was Professor Snape!
Suddenly Harry apparated, he had done it! *I'm so amazing*, thought Harry.

James Delaney (9)
Leadenham CE Primary School, Lincoln

Dangerous Dragon

The mysterious figure of blood-red, deathly black and enchanted-brown immediately transformed into a beastly serpent. Everyone let out an ear-piercing shrill of astonishment and surprise. The foe let out a deep roar, which echoed in and out of people's sensitive ears. 'Surrender yourselves,' hissed the dragon.

Ben Mott (8)
Leadenham CE Primary School, Lincoln

The Legend Of The Demon Shape-Shifter

One day there was a boy called Joe. He spotted a cat. What he didn't know was that it was a demon. He took it home.
Joe played with the demon for one year then it happened … slowly it crept. *Wham!* The bloodthirsty creature got him.
Joe had been killed!

Charlie Cade (8)
Leadenham CE Primary School, Lincoln

What's That Noise?

Glunk! Bang! 'Ohh!'
Calum came home. Calum muttered to himself,
'It's just my imagination.'
He heard it again.
His mum called him inside.
Afterwards, Calum briskly opened the garage
door. He saw a green figure, he heard it mutter,
'I feel sick.' It was The Grinch.

Kelsey MacBain (9)
Leadenham CE Primary School, Lincoln

One Scary Night

It was dark and eerie, everywhere was still, everyone was sleeping except a little boy … he heard a very scary noise. 'Argh!' he screamed, too terrified to look, he opened an eye, and what was revealed was a terrifying monster that stared him in the eye hard.

Eleanor Hall (9)
Leadenham CE Primary School, Lincoln

Alien Invasion

One night it was damp, cold and dark. There was a flying saucer in the air. No one was around on the street … *boom!* A bomb was spectacularly fired at our planet, Earth. Everyone screamed and ran around in circles. The aliens had landed …

Luca Simeoli-Brown (9)
Leadenham CE Primary School, Lincoln

The Fly Who Won Wimbledon

Strategic sporting event. Audience captivated and enthralled, as if they were on the edge of a cliff. Commentators soliloquizing; preparing the suspense. Suddenly, serving at 200mph, creature of magnificence Sharapova versus Fly. B Fly with a match point taking rackets in hand. For the first time a fly won Wimbledon!

Jessica Everett (11)
Leadenham CE Primary School, Lincoln

Potato Wars

The general limped across the battlefield with a peeled leg searching everywhere for at least one survivor. Knives falling, trying to finish the peeling job on the general. Then he saw one of his team, then a knife stabbed straight through him. The general then shared the same fate.
Splat!

Matty Williams (11)
Leadenham CE Primary School, Lincoln

The Mysterious Person

Standing in the corner was a mysterious person who was making the scariest noise anyone could ever imagine. Then the mysterious person started walking towards me, it was like the most frightening time of my life.
Later on, I appeared to be laying on the floor.

Rhianna Jackson (10)
Leadenham CE Primary School, Lincoln

Return Of Medusa

A familiar hissing sound arose from each and every corner of the arched room. A sly figure seemed to just merge in with the walls, copying my every move. In a hoarse whisper the creature cried, 'I am alive but dying, blink and you die!' I blinked …

Emily Mott (9)
Leadenham CE Primary School, Lincoln

War Of The Roast Dinner

The king carrot walked proudly towards the giant cauliflower. He drew his spud grenade and blew the cauliflower to shreds, the carrot's allies floated along the gravy shooting spuds at enemy bread. They dropped the roast potato, it shot towards the bread. *Bang!* The bread was exterminated.

Henry Newton (11)
Leadenham CE Primary School, Lincoln

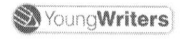

The Last Day Of The World

The curled up head moved as life was inserted, it stood with a *clank!* It said robotically, 'Destroy!' It opened its mouth so its throat blaster was visible. It fired around rapidly, destroying the door. It flew onto the ammunition bed. *Buzz! Boom!* It exploded and with it the world!

Wilf Chapman-Gandy (9)
Leadenham CE Primary School, Lincoln

A Magic Horse

Once upon a time there lived two horses in an enchanted wood, one was about to have a foal. Elizabeth was her name. She was very gorgeous indeed! Her husband was smart, and was always there when she needed him. She finally had the foal. It gave her magic powers.

Rebecca Holland (9)
Leadenham CE Primary School, Lincoln

The Creep

It was the middle of the night as I was walking through the streets. There was a noise in the background. I stopped but there was no one there. I carried on walking. All of a sudden a loud *bang!* and then someone jumped out at me …

Lee Trigg (11)
Maltby Redwood J&I School, Rotherham

The Thing

The woods were dark, the car was cold. I saw something move … again and again. The car came to a stop, we had hit something, we had hit the thing! Dad got out of the car. 'Oh no!' he exclaimed. Was it a monster or … a poor little baby fox?

Oliver Smith (11)
Maltby Redwood J&I School, Rotherham

What Do I Do?

It's dark, I had nowhere to turn. Should I or not? I ran through the trees and bushes. I stopped. I could hear it getting louder. 'Zach, Zach?' It's Bob. 'Oh hi, I thought you were something or someone else!'

Oliver Connolly (11)
Maltby Redwood J&I School, Rotherham

The Joker

Matthew was playing football. Matthew fell over. Fred whispered, 'Have a nice trip.' Fred kicked the ball and Matthew went to get it off the road. Suddenly a car coming round the corner hit Matthew. Fred called an ambulance.
Sadly when Matthew got out of hospital he was seriously disabled.

Thomas Westwood (11)
Maltby Redwood J&I School, Rotherham

Into The Woods

Bang!
'Damn, the wheel's popped, I'm getting out and going into the woods.' So Nick got out, running into the woods for help.
Hours later, banging noises sounded, Sue daren't move. Seeing lights, hearing voices, Sue got out, turned round and saw a man with Nick's head on the axe.

Lyle Copley (11)
Maltby Redwood J&I School, Rotherham

A Forest Nightmare

I walked through the forest then heard footsteps coming towards me. I looked around the corner, there stood a real dinosaur eating leaves off a tree. I stood a bit closer, the dinosaur heard me and looked around … I ran into a bush so it wouldn't see me!

Laura Martin (11)
Maltby Redwood J&I School, Rotherham

Is It A Monster?

It was getting closer, the noise was getting louder. Suddenly the rumbling stopped … but had it stopped? Suddenly it started again, but scarier. I could sense the danger. Suddenly it stopped again but had it? Yes. 'Excuse me Ben, I need to get to the washing machine,' said Mum.

Samuel Shore (11)
Maltby Redwood J&I School, Rotherham

Run!

I shouldn't have let it out. Now I'm running for my life, I'm out of breath, there's only a matter of time till it devours me to shreds. I've got to … *argh!* Now I can only feel a slight warmth on my cheek …
Suddenly I wake up to find a …

Ewan Brown (11)
Maltby Redwood J&I School, Rotherham

School From Hell

The building was cold and deserted. Kevin felt a chill running down his spine whilst creeping down the corridor. The rooms were dark, like someone had spread a blanket over them. He heard footsteps approaching. Kevin entered a room to find someone glaring down at him ... Kevin hated school.

Charlotte Hosier (11)
Maltby Redwood J&I School, Rotherham

A Bad Dream

I stood at the side of the road waiting for a gap in the traffic so I could cross. I walked out, looked up, a car was coming towards me, the driver looking at something else. I was stunned and couldn't move. The car came closer. Suddenly, *'Jim!'* Mum yelled.

Beth Anderson (11)
Maltby Redwood J&I School, Rotherham

The Giant Dog

There was a loud thud as a rock boomed next to Annie's feet. She screamed in terror. A giant dog tried to bite her. She screamed again. *'Annie get up.* Milo stop trying to bite Annie,' said her mum angrily at Milo as he pounced on her. 'Time for school.'

Kathryn Essex (11)
Maltby Redwood J&I School, Rotherham

The Night Ride

I could feel the wind gushing against my face. Faster, faster, spinning round and round. The old rusty tracks shaking me back and forth, now slowly coming to a halt. Stepping out of the carriage, still shivering from the fright of the old rusty railway ride, late on Saturday night.

Eleanor Hill (10)
Maltby Redwood J&I School, Rotherham

Monster Day

Silently he watched the monster gobble his lunch. He knew if he made a tiny noise he would be supper.
The monster roared, he had been spotted.
'Run for it!' shouted Dave.
He ran into the white cave, he heard footsteps.
'Come out of there with your shoes on!'

Mitchell Parker (11)
Maltby Redwood J&I School, Rotherham

Holiday From Hell

A cold chill ran down my spine. I was alone in the hotel. It was quiet … *Bang!* What was that? I started running. Suddenly a man appeared wearing a cape. He started running towards me. I was petrified. 'Help!' No one answered. Everyone had gone. I was alone with Dracula.

Karen Glaves (11)
Maltby Redwood J&I School, Rotherham

The Hot Dog

One day a mad scientist called Bob was experimenting when a green puff of smoke appeared and out came a hot dog. With a slow swaying pace it moved towards its victim. Suddenly, a scream came from Bob's mouth. He woke up and told himself it was all a dream.

Thomas Shore (11)
Maltby Redwood J&I School, Rotherham

Ghost Ride

Sitting in a carriage, my seat jerks. I go flying, landing back on my seat. A slimy feeling shivers down my spine. Suddenly I spin round and round. I find myself in mid-air. The ride eventually ends. I decide to never go on that ride again.

Courtney Bowen (11)
Methodist J&I School, Wakefield

Twinkle, Twinkle, Chocolate Bar

Twinkle, twinkle, chocolate bar, I will find you near or far. Eat your brain and eat your guts, I love you so I go nuts. Twinkle, twinkle, chocolate bar, waiting for me in the car. I'll strip you clean and eat you mean, slipping into the food machine.

William Hirst (11)
Methodist J&I School, Wakefield

Time

I fasten myself in, close my eyes tight and soar into the stars. My journey of time has begun. Where to? The end of the world, but my journey is disturbed by a loud ring. My alarm goes off. It is time to end my exciting journey, for now!

Beth Goldthorpe (11)
Methodist J&I School, Wakefield

Ghost Train

Dark and spooky, my sister and I were shaking. Then all of a sudden, *'Boo!'* A skeleton popped out in front of our faces. We were grasping on to each other's hands then we moved on. I could see daylight.
I wish I had never got on the ghost train!

Matthew Stephenson (10)
Methodist J&I School, Wakefield

A Strange Monster

I heard a strange noise downstairs. I went to investigate, step by step, creak by creak. I went down the stairs. I peered around the corner and there stood a hideous monster. I jumped back with fear. The monster saw me … then my alarm clock went off.

Aidan Piper (10)
Methodist J&I School, Wakefield

First Day

It was my first day at school. My mum dropped me off. A weird tall giant made her way towards me. Her giant sausage fingers beckoned me to go to her desk. I was trapped until I realised that she was my new teacher. I had been such a fool!

Charlotte Clarkson (11)
Methodist J&I School, Wakefield

The Disaster Clock

I lay sleeping, calm in my bed, dreaming away like a little angel. Something flashed in my sleep then it went off. Oh no, the disaster clock rang. I had to get up for my new high school. It was my first day, wicked!

Rio Shaw (11)
Methodist J&I School, Wakefield

Nursery

Sitting quietly in the corner I watched the creature slither towards me. There was no way out. It got closer. I ran to the door, it wouldn't open. A swarm of monsters surrounded me. One monster took me away.
'Come and have your milk now, Holly,' said Mrs Wooton again!'

Holly Holt (11)
Methodist J&I School, Wakefield

Little Red Riding Hood

I skipped to Grandma's. It was hot. Grandma was poorly.
The naughty wolf had put Grandma in the cupboard. I shouted, 'What a big nose you have!'
'All the better to smell you with,' he said.
Daddy saved Grandma. Bye-bye wolf.

Dale Clark, Melissa McDade & Catherine Aylward (11)
Methodist J&I School, Wakefield

The Three Little Pigs

Three little pigs built houses of different materials. Straw, sticks and bricks. A wolf came and tried to blow all the houses down but could not blow down the house of brick. All the pigs were safe but the wolf didn't survive.

Alex Luo (11)
Methodist J&I School, Wakefield

Titanic

On its first voyage the liner Titanic hit a huge iceberg. It broke in half and unfortunately lots of people died in the freezing water. It sank quickly to the bottom of the deep sea. Recently some divers went down and discovered most of the wreck of the great liner.

Shannon Dickinson (11)
Methodist J&I School, Wakefield

The Loch Ness Monster And Me

I was staring at Loch Ness lake. It was calm. Suddenly the Loch Ness monster burst out of the surface and dragged me to my watery grave where I also became a small human-like sea monster and dragged my evil brother down as well.

Jacob Earnshaw (10)
Methodist J&I School, Wakefield

Merlin Gets Eaten

Merlin was practising a fire wave spell on dummies at the magicians' training room. Suddenly his magic staff failed and a flash of light occurred. Immediately a yeti burst out of the ground, ate Merlin and became a magic yeti.

He conquered the world and no one could stop him.

Max Holman (10)
Methodist J&I School, Wakefield

The Haircut

Linda boiled, her powers created smoke and smell and *puff!* nothing happened. She had forgotten to say the magic words.
She started again. 'Please cut his hair, cut his hair nice and fair.' *Puff!* A book? 'Oh no, not again. All I want to do is cut his hair!'

Kimberley Dudley (11)
Methodist J&I School, Wakefield

Nobody There

I arrived at school but there was no sign of life. I walked round the playground, there was nobody there. I looked in the windows, the classrooms were bare. Then I felt stupid. My head clicked. I'd forgotten to put my watch back an hour, I was an hour early.

Elliott Armitage (11)
Methodist J&I School, Wakefield

Space Freaks

It was a normal day until an alien ship landed on the school. A blob came out and ate the President of the USA.

The military came to shoot the blob: it didn't work. They tried missile launchers. It didn't stop it. Then someone blew it up.

Lewis Short (10)
Micklefield CE Primary School, Leeds

The Enchanted Book

Leon, Vinny and Emilio were stuck inside on a rainy day. They were bored so went into the loft to find some books to read. Vinny found an old book and they went into the room to read it. They opened the book and went whizzing off to dragon land.

John Bland (10)
Micklefield CE Primary School, Leeds

Most Haunted

I was coming from school, I saw a dead person so I ran home. I tried to unlock the door but it was locked with the other key. So I climbed through the window. I heard someone scream so I ran downstairs, my family were dead! *No!*

Ashley Sylvester (11)
Micklefield CE Primary School, Leeds

An Odd Day Out

A girl called Gemma went to a mansion. She walked in, the door shut behind her. She heard a moaning and groaning sound. Suddenly she was swooped off the ground and taken away somewhere. She ran out of the mansion but there was just a big black hole.

Emma Gledhill (10)
Micklefield CE Primary School, Leeds

The Trip To The Seaside

Once there was a little girl called Katie who was going to the seaside, Scarborough. When she got there she went on the beach for a bit, then she went next door to the horror house. She was really scared because her family were being chased with an axe.

Jessica Melia (10)
Micklefield CE Primary School, Leeds

Friday Night Tragedy

It was 8pm, training had finished and I was getting changed into my clean clothes when I heard a scream. I quickly put on my socks and trainers and got on my bike. I rode out of the ground and got to the main road and a car had

...

Ryan White (11)
Micklefield CE Primary School, Leeds

Sharapova V Jancovic

Sharapova had just won a tournament she'd been training for. Nervous to find it was raining really heavily she was extremely disappointed it had to be cancelled.

Sharapova met Jancovic again. Sharapova found it a struggle but she managed to pull through and win! She shouted, 'Come on!'

Libby Jones (10)
Micklefield CE Primary School, Leeds

The Magic Fairy Tree

One day a girl called Mary and a boy called James decided to go for a walk. Mary saw a big tree so James climbed the tree.
'Careful James.'
'I'll be fine.'
Suddenly the tree wobbled.
'Watch out!'
James fell to the ground.
'Oi,' said a voice.
'Look, a fairy!'

Charlotte Keeble (11)
Micklefield CE Primary School, Leeds

Aliens

One ordinary day a spaceship was launched. When it got in space everyone felt rumbling. The top guards were looking for the self-destruct button. They found it but were attacked by aliens. They killed them. They then pressed the self-destruct button and escaped in an escape pod.

Adam Saunders (10)
Micklefield CE Primary School, Leeds

Hallowe'en Night

Izzy wakes up. Her room is in total darkness. She hears a terrifying sound. Izzy worries and starts to shout, 'Mum? Dad?' Nobody replies. She sees a white mist floating up the landing. Izzy runs downstairs straight into the closet. A massive spider is on her shoulder. It is Hallowe'en.

Georgia Hargrave (10)
Micklefield CE Primary School, Leeds

How The Ice Age Occurred

'Hades, you stole my wife and daughter you shall pay. I'll freeze the Underworld for 40 days and 40 nights.'

Eventually Hades gave up and gave back Zeus' wife and daughter. Zeus stopped the freeze. This is how the Ice Age occurred and ended.

Jacob Hird (10)
Northstead CP School, Scarborough

Zeus' Revenge

Hades stole all the gods' food and Zeus' family. Zeus wanted revenge so he flooded the Underworld then threw salt over the water for the seas.

Next he made an earthquake, which made the mountains.

Finally he threw warm and cold winds together to form a tornado.

Katie Wallace
Northstead CP School, Scarborough

The Sun And The Rain

'How could you do this?' said Zeus. Hades had stolen Zeus' daughter! Zeus had a plan. He was going to melt Hades' people with a blinding light, the sun …
In doing this he killed his daughter!
Every time it rains it is Zeus crying over the loss of his daughter!

Rachel Head
Northstead CP School, Scarborough

The Day I Stood In A Magical Puddle

Zeus stood in a puddle but the water expanded and turned into a river with fish swimming, birds singing and leaves floating.
After a while a huge waterfall led into the river. People then said they would call it the River Zeus.

Jordan Hookem
Northstead CP School, Scarborough

Ice In Canada

It was a fine day, then Hades came and stole the blade of Olympus, Zeus was furious! He was so mad that he froze the whole of North Bay (Canada). Hades begged for mercy and gave the blade back to Zeus immediately. That is why people camp on North Bay.

Esme Ripley
Northstead CP School, Scarborough

Water

Hades stole Zeus' first son, Diametes! Hades tortured Diametes with his whip. All the gods wept and wept and wept … they wept so much that it caused rain and rain and more rain, which created oceans and seas and rivers and lakes that twisted down the world like raging snakes!

Isaac Wilsher
Northstead CP School, Scarborough

How Mountains Were Made

It was a fine day, it seemed, until the blade of Olympus went missing.
Around 1 hour later a letter came through the enormous door. It was from Hades, the king of the Underworld. Zeus sent terrible lightning to kill Hades and the lightning made the mountains.

Joe Eaveson
Northstead CP School, Scarborough

The Battle Of Gods

Hades stole Zeus' crown. Zeus sent his knights to get Hades, Hades sent the knights back. This went on and on and this is how the tides were created - backwards and forwards. Zeus also kicked the world in temper and that is why the Earth is tilted on its axis.

Molly Sheader (10)
Northstead CP School, Scarborough

Day Appears

Night was on Earth. The Sun Goddess appeared. She tried and tried but couldn't form the sun. Afterwards Zeus appeared. 'You're the wrong person, arise the Star Goddess,' spoke Zeus.

Out from nowhere came the Star Goddess from light. The Star Goddess made stars to form the sun and day.

Zachary Slater
Northstead CP School, Scarborough

How Mount Everest Was Made

Hades had stolen the Olympus coin from Zeus. Zeus was very angry and challenged Hades to a battle. Hades accepted the challenge. At the end Zeus pulled a humungous chunk from the ground and piled it on Hades and by doing so he created Mount Everest.

Ben Foster
Northstead CP School, Scarborough

How Rivers Came To The Earth

Running wild, running free with ribbons in her hair and a dress of pearls. Suddenly a beautiful, silky ribbon fell on the grass slithering and sliding, turning into a river. The beautiful Goddess of Water saw what happened and threw lots of ribbons all over the world and created rivers.

Hayley Towell
Northstead CP School, Scarborough

The Battle

A long, long time ago in Greece on some rocky hills there was a great city called Athens. A Greek army was unleashed but nearby there was an army that followed Troy. The following day there was a battle, a gory battle. The Battle of Troy.

Sam Hepples
Northstead CP School, Scarborough

How Lakes And Seas Came To The World!

Zeus was standing there with his eyes filled with tears! Hades had killed Athena. There was no love anymore: Zeus was mad. He attacked Hades for six months without stopping! Hades was so upset he cried for ages and that is how lakes and seas were formed!

Ella Whelan
Northstead CP School, Scarborough

How Volcanoes Were Made!

Athena took some buns. On top were strawberries for her father. But then she tripped and the buns fell down to Earth. This created volcanoes, the strawberries melted, causing lava and the seeds created stones. That's how volcanoes were created.

Amy Potton
Northstead CP School, Scarborough

The Dark Sea

Crash! Crash! The waves powered their way against the water.
I sat on the sea wall, looking out over the storm. The power was down but one light still shone in the bay. It was an eerie light; it moved rapidly closer. Suddenly a shape loomed out of the abyss …

Joshua Walker (11)
Otley All Saints CE Primary School, Leeds

A Comsognathus Comes Back to Life

Splash! I was soaked with a gooey slime. It clung between my toes. Weird noises echoed through the barred tunnels of sludge. I kept running. The darkness closed me into a sinister blanket. I smelt something different, human. I decided to head for the smell, they could lead me out!

Hal Laverty (11)
Otley All Saints CE Primary School, Leeds

Bob's Birthday

'Fantastic!' shouted Bob. 'I love it. Thanks, Mum!' It was Bob's birthday and he'd got a new bike. The bike had big chunky wheels with extra grip on, it was a bright ruby-red and it sparkled like a diamond. Bob rushed outside to ride his bike and fell off …

Louis Cook (11)
Otley All Saints CE Primary School, Leeds

Treasure Beach

Beep! Beep! went the metal detector. 'Wow what was that?' said George.
'It was a treasure,' yelled Norman.
'Let's dig it up,' George said.
For the next ten minutes they dug.
'We've found it,' shouted George. When they opened the chest they found it full of jewels.
'We're rich!' cried Norman.

Leo Hannan (11)
Otley All Saints CE Primary School, Leeds

Mischievous Friend

Walking home from school I saw my best friend walking with her so-called worst enemy. I called her name quite loudly. She looked round and I scarcely heard what she said but I think I heard, 'Meet you at eight.' I paused, wondering why she would say that …

Afnan Ezzeldin (11)
Otley All Saints CE Primary School, Leeds

What Was That?

The sun was going down in Barnoldswick. Lily was just tiredly trudging up the stairs when there was a loud thudding noise about a metre behind her. Lily didn't know what to do! Thinking quickly she ran up the stairs and grabbed a nearby phone. Quickly she rang her mum …

Grace Pollard (11)
Otley All Saints CE Primary School, Leeds

In the Park At 9pm

I was on the street at 9pm in the park. I was sat there shivering. The swings were moving, the roundabout going round and round, the chains squeaking, somebody was sniffing among the darkness. I turned around and somebody grabbed my shoulder. 'Argh!' I screamed. They grabbed me harder. 'Help!'

Sophie Elliott (10)
Otley All Saints CE Primary School, Leeds

A Day In The Life Of A Dolphin!

How amazing! I swapped bodies with a dolphin. How cool! I swam all day, leapt in and out of the water. I ate some fish. *Yum!* I swam with the other dolphins. It was really warm; it was in Spain. I wonder if the dolphin enjoyed it in my body?

Tegan Senior (11)
Otley All Saints CE Primary School, Leeds

Drama!

Drama, drama, drama! They were the words floating through my head. It was the real thing. The play: Joseph and I were brothers. My heart was pumping. I was a brother about to go on stage …

Ha, the play is done! There was no trouble at all, just nerves!

Olivia White (11)
Otley All Saints CE Primary School, Leeds

Ben's Song

Ben was a great guitarist, he was so good he could kill! His 1990s Les Paul style guitar played such a sad tune everyone died except Ben's dad.

He crept up to his father's room, raised the guitar above his head and, his dad shouted, 'Stop, boy. Treat that guitar better!'

Oliver Proctor (11)
Otley All Saints CE Primary School, Leeds

A Nightmare?

Sam woke at 2am. There was a thunderstorm. Rain was hitting the roof of Sam's bedroom. Sam got out of bed and looked out of the window. *What in the world was that?* It was the Grim Reaper! It saw him and ran off. How had it got there?

James Gardner (11)
Otley All Saints CE Primary School, Leeds

It's Coming …

'Argh!'
I was screaming like mad! I'd just seen it running quickly down the deserted place. It was coming closer. I kept very still, trying not to move, but I couldn't contain myself. I ran screaming down the road. Then I saw it again. The rabbit running down the road.

Emma Tranter (11)
Otley All Saints CE Primary School, Leeds

Jim And His Thoughts

Jim was strolling down a dark thicket when he heard footsteps from behind. He turned round, there was no one there. He started getting worried. Jim carried on walking. He heard voices shouting, 'Jim, is that you?'
Jim thought, *I have heard those voices,* he turned. It was his parents.

Joe Scott (11)
Rawmarsh Monkwood Junior School, Rawmarsh

In The Pet Shop

One gloomy day, Samuel and his mum were walking in the woods. Suddenly, a cave appeared through the trees. 'Look Mum, a cave,' exclaimed Samuel.
They stepped inside the cave and saw a dragon with ruby-red eyes.
'Is this the rat you want to buy?' said Mum.

Samuel James
St Andrew's CE Primary School, Leasingham

The Evil Teacher

Running, sprinting, gasping for breath. Sweat dripping off his head.
Jamie was terrified he had missed his maths class!

Jack Whalen (10)
St Andrew's CE Primary School, Leasingham

Tears Of The Damned

Insides screaming; I couldn't feel my trembling fingers. My vision hazy, blurred by salty tears. We lined up like we were about to be shot. My heart vigorously pumping, sweat trickling down my scarred forehead. Alone, left to die. The agonising, excruciating, sound filled sore ears. Not geography class again!

Emily Robinson (11)
St Andrew's CE Primary School, Leasingham

The Big Jump

The moment of truth, this was it, a 10,000-feet cliff. I was going to jump off the cliff. It was dark. I couldn't see the bottom. No parachute, I just had a T-shirt and shorts. Suddenly I jumped. 'Stop playing on the kerb, it's teatime,' Mum yelled.

Keely McNiffe
St Andrew's CE Primary School, Leasingham

Bedtime

The bed looms before me, I creep in holding my breath. I reach up towards the light, click the night light switch on.
'Just get into bed, it's bedtime.'
'OK,' I say.
The quilt closes in around me like a snake. I kick, I scream. My mum comes in.

Nathan Carne (11)
St Andrew's CE Primary School, Leasingham

Darkness

I slowly tiptoed down the old squeaky stairs with sweat dripping down my forehead, I opened the door. Suddenly I saw darkness. I walked forwards, all I could feel on my bare feet was the soft carpet, then I saw it … the tree. 'Fred, get away from the Christmas tree.'

Danny Ward (11)
St Andrew's CE Primary School, Leasingham

The Crunch

Cautiously I opened the ancient door. Horror-struck I saw my mum, Debbie, crouching in the corner of the room sobbing like a catastrophic disaster had occurred! Between guilty sobs she confessed her crime. 'I'm a mu-mu-murderer!' she cried.
'Who was the victim?' I questioned.
'Sammy the snail!' she cried.

Robert Wiles (11)
St Andrew's CE Primary School, Leasingham

Daredevil

'The great daredevil, Thomas Warrenton, is about to jump off the 20ft mountain.'
My heart started to tremble. I took a deep breath, walked to the edge of the cliff. My eyes started to wobble.
'Hurry up, hurry up,' fans chanted. 'Thomas, Thomas, hurry up, come on, just jump!'

Lauren Culpan (10)
St Andrew's CE Primary School, Leasingham

Anticipation

I opened the door … The hustle and bustle of the art block nearly knocked me over! I had knots in my stomach. I felt dizzy and sick. Adrenaline was being pumped around my body. It was a powerful thing. Walking in I saw the new teacher who had just arrived.

Leah Hammatt (11)
St Andrew's CE Primary School, Leasingham

Untitled

This was the moment, the daredevil was about to jump the highest ramp in the world. It was so high that the audience had to stand at least 100 feet away. Fast, furious, the daredevil was. A dash came upon my face, Fred had gotten up the curb.

Alex Dickinson
St Andrew's CE Primary School, Leasingham

Untitled

One day I could hear the evil thing creeping up my jail door. It sounded like it was spreading a message. The jail door opened and the thing got in … *argh!*
'Mum, do you have to wake me up?'

Charlene Cowap (11)
St Andrew's CE Primary School, Leasingham

The Deathly Jump

A deathly silence was broken, someone shouted, 'Are you going to do it?' He was too scared to even notice. He sat down on the edge and looked down. It must be miles down, or so he thought. This was it, he jumped.
Splash! Safely in the pool!

Chloë Banks (11)
St Andrew's CE Primary School, Leasingham

Bottomless

Here I am at the edge of the bottomless pit. I cannot see anything as it is blurred. In a few seconds I will dive in … here I go. *Splash!* All I did was dive in the pool, how terrible to get wrinkles!

Zak Smith (11)
St Andrew's CE Primary School, Leasingham

Untitled

'Run,' shouted the Doctor while running from a tall Dalek.
'Exterminate,' shouted a Dalek.
Quickly, the Doctor opened the TARDIS time machine's doors. The Dalek pulled the laser and hit the Doctor …
'Wake up, Bob,' shouted his mum.

Sam Boughton (11)
St Andrew's CE Primary School, Leasingham

Danger Or Not!

Running. Panting and gasping for breath a girl was being swiftly pursued into a forest by a lion. The girl was seven years old, she wore a golden dress (with no shoes). As she was running towards a wall, she heard …
'Get out of bed!' shouted Mum.

Megan Curnow (11)
St Andrew's CE Primary School, Leasingham

Party With My Soul Mates

A spaceship landed in my back garden.
It shrank down and flew into my bedroom, four
aliens came and took me to Jupiter.
I saw Elvis Presley, MichaelAngelo, a Viking,
King Henry VIII and Queen Victoria.
They had a party for me. Am I dead?
I woke up.

Claire Saxby (7)
St Andrews Junior School, Brighouse

My Dog Has A Big Tail

My dog has a big tail and is very annoying.
One day a robber broke into the house.
My dog was mopping up the floor and I thought
he was a nuisance but his big tail hit the robber.
He fell to the ground, I love my dog's tail.

Annalie Pearson (8)
St Andrews Junior School, Brighouse

That Feeling

This is my worst fear.
My face is stinging, stomach churning, hair flying, hands shaking, feet sprinting.
I cannot slow down.
Trees whizzing past.
Plunging down, down, down, landing with a crash at the bottom.
I wish I didn't get that feeling when I run down a hill.

Liberty Hodgson (8)
St Andrews Junior School, Brighouse

A Bizarre Experiment

Once there was a man called Boomer, he was a scientist in Hong Kong.
One day Boomer put a wrong liquid in a glass and suddenly *boom!* There was a big explosion, nearly every glass exploded, Boomer was shaken by his laboratory.
He nearly lost his own job.
It's terrible.

Bradley Mason
St Andrews Junior School, Brighouse

Two Brave Knights

One day two brave knights called St Jamie and St Thomas went to the centre of Manchester and they saw people running.
St Jamie asked one person and he said, *'That!'*
St Jamie and St Thomas ran at the ugly monster.
They both killed the monster in one piece.

Jamie Browne (8)
St Andrews Junior School, Brighouse

Messy Millie

Messy Millie was messy, everyone said so.
Millie didn't care.
One day Millie said she was going to be clean, so she folded up her nightdress. Her mum didn't notice. Millie was mad about this, she kept on trying. It was no good so she went back to being messy!

Bethany Knight (8)
St Andrews Junior School, Brighouse

The Adventures Of Max And Connor

Max and Connor went to a magic show. The wizard put them in a time machine. They went to the future. They saw a scary alien, with massive claws. It tried to cut them up. They ran back to the time machine.
Where would they end up next?

Jack Barraclough (8)
St Andrews Junior School, Brighouse

Untitled

One day the RAF went to a problem on the coast.
HMS Victory was sinking, it had been hit by a rock. The RAF got the men out and the helicopter sprayed water on the ship. The fire boats did the same. Then they took the ship back to shore.

Edward Priestley (8)
St Andrews Junior School, Brighouse

Nicky And Sarah's Mystery

Nicky and Sarah were on a walk.
They heard a magical sound. Then a fairy put a spell on them.
Suddenly they turned into frogs. They couldn't believe their eyes. How would they get out of that state?
The fairy disappeared. Suddenly they went back to normal.

Jade Littlewood (8)
St Andrews Junior School, Brighouse

Fire In The Forest

Jamie and Jessica were walking in the forest. They came to an old broken bridge. Under the old broken bridge there was quicksand. Jamie and Jessica ran across it quickly. They came to a forest. The forest was on fire. They ran quickly home. Mum and Dad were happy.

Charlotte Hopley (8)
St Andrews Junior School, Brighouse

The Magic Food

Jack and John were going to magic some food.
They started to do a trick. Jack did his spell,
'Abracadabra, can you bring food?'
But it didn't come.
John tried his trick, 'Abracadabra, I want some food!'
The food came and they were happy.

Damian Wales (8)
St Andrews Junior School, Brighouse

The Haunted House

One day Anne moved into a new house. She found out a strange man had died there. At night a vampire popped up from nowhere. She was scared and ran out of the room. It all went pitch-dark. When the light came back oh, she was in her bed.

Lochlan Graham (8)
St Andrews Junior School, Brighouse

The Fire Of The Wood

Tom and Harry went for a walk in a wood. They were talking when they heard a noise. It was a fire!
They ran to a bridge and found a bucket and got some water. They put out the fire. Then they carried on talking about football.

Thomas Metcalfe
St Andrews Junior School, Brighouse

Nasty Sisters

A little girl called Sparkle lived in a palace.
She cast a spell. She had two ugly sisters who
never let her play or go out, but one day she
said, 'I don't have to do what you say.'
The sisters replied, 'OK.'
They stopped being nasty. They were friends.

Holly Kitteringham (7)
St Andrews Junior School, Brighouse

The Three Polar Bears

Three polar bears lived in an old house under a tree.
They were eating cornflakes when Duck knocked on the door. He invited Little Polar Bear to his party. He couldn't go. Little Polar Bear was sad, so his mum changed her mind. The party was great fun.

Millie Clegg (8)
St Andrews Junior School, Brighouse

Monster

I am scared of something, something very bad. Something I thought wasn't real, just made-up. I bet you would laugh at it if you heard it. It happens where I sleep. When I look under my bed I see two eyes. I told my mum. She looked. Two marbles!

Zara Dunford (9)
St Hilda's School, Wakefield

Alone

I came home from school. The door was open and the lights were switched off. I turned on the light and searched the house but as soon as I turned around, there was Santa. 'Happy Birthday! Your parents are coming, they got stuck in a traffic jam,' said Santa.

Elizabeth Grimes (9)
St Hilda's School, Wakefield

Scared

I was setting off to a party. I thought I was late so I decided to go through the park. It was a shortcut.
In the park I got really scared because I could hear noises. I ran as fast as I could. I was early. Oh no!

Abigail Edson (9)
St Hilda's School, Wakefield

Surprise Happy Birthday Party

It was dark and quiet. You could only hear the wind and rain. There was nobody there to be seen. Then there was a noise like a crack in another room. So she walked in. There was no noise and then there was a surprise birthday party for her!

Isabel Kaye (9)
St Hilda's School, Wakefield

Tiny Tales Yorkshire & Lincolnshire

Doctor Mad

'Joan, bring me my test tubes and my formula. Right, I think we're almost done! Just a little bit of this and then I think we're there. Joan! Come here! I've finished. I'm calling it Dumbo the Elephant.'

'I spent my time doing this to make a stupid elephant!'

Amelia Wain (9)
St Hilda's School, Wakefield

The Haunted House

I turned around. I saw nothing but I felt a knot in my stomach. I was alone. No one was around me. All I could see were lots of flights of stairs. I went upstairs. I saw a coffin. I opened it and from it came a dead person …

Zoya Karim (9)
St Hilda's School, Wakefield

A Scary Trip

On our school trip to Oakwell Hall, Mistress Pauline was our guide for the day. She wore traditional Tudor clothes and had a greyness in her face. As she told us the story about the ghost of William Batt, she flickered in the dim light, until suddenly completely gone! Vanished!

Kyrie McConnell (8)
St Hilda's School, Wakefield

Too Busy For Love

Mrs Vet had many children, animals and patients, but no time or a husband. She felt lonely. She fell in love with a lighthouse keeper but had no time to see him.
One day the doorbell rang. The lighthouse keeper stood there holding a poorly pigeon. They both smiled.

Katie Crowther (8)
St Hilda's School, Wakefield

Ruby's Horror

I was on my bed, Mum called, 'Ruby get up!' I plodded down into the kitchen. *Aarrgh!* My teacher, Mrs Llewgrun, was sitting at the kitchen table. She told me an awful story about a robber that smashed her house down. Was she lying and checking I'd done my homework?

Annabelle Brook (7)
St Hilda's School, Wakefield

Earthquake

The sky went dark and the birds fell silent. I felt a tremble beneath my feet. My body shook as the earth opened beneath me. I tumbled downwards. Down into the blackness. I was doomed. I screamed, 'Help!'
My teacher said, 'What on earth is the matter, Tilly? Daydream?'

Tilly Nicholls (8)
St Hilda's School, Wakefield

The Haunted House

I walked in, I was scared. It was my first time in a haunted house. There were scary noises all around me but I kept on walking through he hallways. I saw a light. I ran to it. I walked in and saw all my friends. It was a trick!

Charlotte Oldroyd (8)
St Hilda's School, Wakefield

I Don't Want To!

When I got there it was horrible. I didn't want to be there. I just wanted to go home, but Mum and Dad made me stay.

The next couple of days there were activities including games, swimming, rock climbing, lots of fun. I'd go again next year to summer camp.

Jennifer Watson (8)
St Hilda's School, Wakefield

Tiny Tales Yorkshire & Lincolnshire

The Helicopter Ride

It began lifting into the air, I looked out of the glass window. I tried to close my eyes but that didn't work. I tried to take deep breaths but when I tried that everybody looked at me. I realised that it had already landed. I was so relieved.

Victoria Newton (8)
St Hilda's School, Wakefield

Loop-The-Loop

My tummy was turning as the roller coaster started to move. It moved slowly up the hill. My hands were shaking with fear. Suddenly I found myself upside down. It felt like I was falling. I didn't know this was no ordinary roller coaster. It was a loop-the-loop.

Paris Mann (8)
St Hilda's School, Wakefield

Super Miracle Shampoo

I'm Hammie the dog who loves ham but I love Minnie more. Minnie is the only dog I know who likes having baths. For her birthday I gave Minnie some super miracle shampoo. By the time she had finished bathing she had turned into a cat!

Maria Brook (7)
St Hilda's School, Wakefield

All By Myself

By myself in a dark corner of the house, suddenly I heard a noise. *Bang! Crash!* Lights started to flash. I screamed, no one came. What was coming towards me? A huge figure in black. No face, just darkness. Then I heard, 'Time for school Olivia.'
What a dream.

Olivia Stead (8)
St Hilda's School, Wakefield

The Cute Rabbit

My mum took me to the pet shop and she put me somewhere. I was really scared. When it was time to go Mum ordered a rabbit. Something was moving at night-time. I went down to see what it was. It was a rabbit. I called it Fluffy. Cute.

Meera Sharma (8)
St Hilda's School, Wakefield

Me And My Pony

I'm sure I'll fall.
'Kick,' yells my teacher.
We begin to canter. Clinging on tightly, trying not to panic. We fly round until it is over and we trot. The lesson ends and I am safely off my pony.
'Ow!' I trip over, cracking my head open on the concrete.

Helena Watford (8)
St Hilda's School, Wakefield

How We Left The Earth

One evening we grazed the plains calmly. The pterodactyls roamed the skies and the air was moist. Then, it all went dark quickly. The sky was closing in and the ground shook. Then, the sky compressed us.

We weren't seen again. The sky created the new land. We're forever … gone.

Sine Kelly (10)
St Mary's Catholic Primary School, Knaresborough

Hanna's Fostering Story

Hanna lived in a foster home, always looking for a family home to live in.

One day a couple named Mr and Mrs Brown came and fostered her. They took her home and Hanna was so happy. This was the best family ever.

She still visited the foster home friends.

Francesca Recchia (10)
St Mary's Catholic Primary School, Knaresborough

Glacey The Polar Bear

There was once a polar bear called Glacey. He loved snow. He always played with the snow, with his friends. They all buried each other and made houses and had snowball fights.
Oh … how they loved snow, they all had happy lives with snow. Their kids loved snow too.

Alexander Ashton-Evans (10)
St Mary's Catholic Primary School, Knaresborough

Holiday

We went on holiday to Cumbria and we climbed a mountain. It was six miles high. Suddenly, a mountain goat went ramming into our dog. She nearly ran off the edge but luckily she was only a puppy and quite weak. It was the best holiday of my life!

Lucy Noctor (9)
St Mary's Catholic Primary School, Knaresborough

Peter And The Dragon

There was a boy called Peter and his hero was his dad because he always saved the day. One day Peter thought as he was his dad's son he could slay a dragon so he decided to march up to one and slay it, but he was eaten straight away.

Rebecca Stockman (10)
St Mary's Catholic Primary School, Knaresborough

The Crash Of Hamilton

Vroom! Hamilton turning round the corner. Alonso bumps him off the course. Hamilton is out of control. My heart is beating fast, he has to win this race.
Vroom! Bang! Noo! He's lost the Formula 1 Monaco Grand Prix.

Jordan Firth (10)
St Mary's Catholic Primary School, Knaresborough

The Wonders Of Water!

I was scuttling along quite happily in my ladybird manner when I came across a reservoir (a puddle to you humans). I scuttled over to it to find a ladybird identical to me drowning helplessly! I decided to save her. I plunged in and she was gone! How strange!

Alice Bryant (10)
St Mary's Catholic Primary School, Knaresborough

Max And The Cat!

Cor blimey look at that!
Max was in the larder and he'd spotted heaven of all heavens a plate of cheese, he ran forwards, as he ran the cat smelt him. It jumped up to eat him. Max ran for his life, back to his hole. Safe!

Libby Owens (10)
St Mary's Catholic Primary School, Knaresborough

The Trapdoor Of Giant Spiders

I was sitting on my table. I noticed something on the floor. I touched it and a trapdoor opened. I went down it. I looked inside and there were giant spiders! I ran for my life. I shut the trapdoor and flopped on my bed. I was safe.

Sabrina Gaertner (10)
St Mary's Catholic Primary School, Knaresborough

May And Max

May was very scared. Max was in the forest somewhere.
'Max, you win, come out now, please, Max.'
There was silence in the forest. A shadowy being crept behind May, 'Boo!'
'Argh!'
It was Max!
Then someone grabbed both of them and said, 'Max and May, tea is ready!'

Charlie Baker (10)
St Mary's Catholic Primary School, Knaresborough

The Weak Sumo Guy

Once there lived a weak man from China called Ryo Hazuki. He was a real weakling and never took big challenges.
One day he took a sumo challenge, against a five hundred-pound man.
I think you guessed, he lost.
He never tried that challenge ever, ever again.

Jordan Tear (10)
St Mary's Catholic Primary School, Knaresborough

The Angry Dog

Once there was a dog who got angry at everything and everyone.
Once there was a cow who went up to him and said, 'You gotta chill dude,' took a necklace from her neck and swung it back and forth. He suddenly became happy and started singing and dancing, 'Hooray!'

Danielle Huggon (10)
St Mary's Catholic Primary School, Knaresborough

The Deadly Vampire

There was a very spooky man who stayed in his house, apart from the dead of night.
He was in his lab when he decided he needed fresh young blood so he gathered all the children and brothers and sisters and sucked their bodies clean of blood.

Jacob Fincham-Dukes (10)
St Mary's Catholic Primary School, Knaresborough

Jack And The Magic Pet

One day Jack woke up and saw a dog in his bedroom, but he noticed it was a magic dog so he ran downstairs and told his mum. His mum was amazed to know.
He looked after the magic pet until it vanished forever!

Kerrie Turner (8)
St Mary's RC Primary School, Boston

A Day In The Park

Once there was a girl called Sophie. This sounds OK but it's just the beginning … Sophie went to the park. She heard something behind her so she turned round and saw a face in a tree. She looked down and saw legs as well. *'Argh!'*
She was never seen again.

Emma Thornalley (9)
St Mary's RC Primary School, Boston

First Day With Charlotte

One day there was a little boy called Jack. It was his first day at school. He couldn't wait! When they got to school Jack went into the classroom and sat down. It was noisy! 'Miss, Miss. Charlotte's pulling my hair,' were his first words.

Niall Larkin (9)
St Mary's RC Primary School, Boston

The Magic Garden

One day at the bottom of my garden was a sparkling blue pond with a tiny bird beside it having a drink. Then it flew away, but it came back and I gave it some bread to eat.
Now I feed the birds every day. It is my magic garden.

Rio Upsall (8)
St Mary's RC Primary School, Boston

Magic Adventure

One day a girl was shopping. She found a pretty stone. She put it in her hand. The stone started glowing, it took her to a magical valley. She was very happy.

Soon she woke up and went back home. She put the stone back where she found it.

Justyna Dombek (9)
St Mary's RC Primary School, Boston

Tiny Tales Yorkshire & Lincolnshire

Rocky Roller Coaster

There we were all strapped in and then we jolted and started - up, down, left, right and backwards. I was trembling like nothing on Earth, my spine tickling an icy tingle and I could hear my little sister screaming. I felt a heart attack. Why did we have to go?

Lucy Nove (9)
Shelf J&I School, Halifax

The Monster

The monster lay in a valley of green mountains. The monster was breathing heavily. The beast woke because of loud thuds getting louder and louder. The monster tried to hide but he couldn't! It came. 'Get out of bed, you're going to be late for school.'

Chester Robinson (11)
Shelf J&I School, Halifax

The Duck

The duck waddled over to the nest filled with twigs and approximately six different textures of leaves. Then the duck fitted herself into place. Hours later she was still sat there but this time with four little balls of fluff. *Quack, quack, quack.*

Cassie Lewis (11)
Shelf J&I School, Halifax

The Beach

Suddenly Jemma was trapped inside the sandcastle. She looked out the window, what had happened? Had she shrunk? Then she saw it, the wave heading towards the sandcastle. She was underwater now … she heard her mum shout at her to get out of the bath.

Jessica Foulds (11)
Shelf J&I School, Halifax

Tiny Tales Yorkshire & Lincolnshire

The Flying Thing

There it was, a flying thing had just come in the house through the open window. I dived behind the couch, *I'm safe here!* I thought.
I slowly peered over the cushion but there it was, coming closer, it was heading for me.
'It's only a tiny bee!' Mum explained.

Rhys Wardman (11)
Shelf J&I School, Halifax

A Girl's Best Friend

My name is Treacle. I'm a dog.
One day I was left by the side of the road.
I was found, washed, fed and watered.
All I needed now was a home and to be loved.
My name is Megan. I have a new dog called
Treacle. I love him.

Megan Lee (8)
Shelf J&I School, Halifax

The Thing

He froze as the thing walked in. Mouth open wide. It looked at him with fiery eyes gleaming with rage.
It sat down with a thud. Then it opened its beastly mouth and said in an evil, crackly, monstrous voice, 'Where's your homework!'

Brodie Wilson (11)
Shelf J&I School, Halifax

The Speaking Tree

There was a boy and he was out walking when he walked past a tree and he heard a whistle, so he looked around, there was nothing.
Suddenly the tree said, 'Hi dude.'
The boy shouted, 'A talking tree!'
'Shush, it's only your imagination.'
Then he woke up screaming!

Bradley Power (10)
Shelf J&I School, Halifax

Tiny Tales Yorkshire & Lincolnshire

Football Practice

The school bell rang. It was time to go home. When I got home it was time for football practice. My mum takes me to practice with a friend. We were ready for the game. The whistle blew. Then I had to go to the doctors.

Dominic Prentice (11)
Shelf J&I School, Halifax

Born To Be A Winner

I skidded round the corner. I was fast as lightning. I couldn't possibly lose.
I overtook the car in front of me and the next one and the next one.
I could see the finish line, I'm going to win!
The chequered flag isn't in the neighbour's wall, is it?

Elliott Parkinson (11)
Shelf J&I School, Halifax

Seagulls

They flew above us, wings beating, beaks clacking, circling lower, eyes narrowed, beaks open. Then they dived, plunging through the sky, straight at us.
Don't let them get your sandwich.

Sebastian Megson (11)
Shelf J&I School, Halifax

The Gunshot

I rolled under the van while my men kept shooting.
I heard silence, I looked out.
My men were all dead and their men were still there looking at me. I was pulled out and handcuffed to a pole, well a flag.
They only said one thing, 'Game over!'

Ashley Stewart (11)
Shelf J&I School, Halifax

Tiny Tales Yorkshire & Lincolnshire

Kitty, Kitty

Kitty, Kitty sat on the wall, Kitty Kitty had a great fall. Down and down the kitty fell, but unfortunately landed in a well.
The kitty landed on a boat and sailed down the well's moat.

Sophie Leek (11)
Shelf J&I School, Halifax

Coming

They were coming, I could sense it. Their voices grew louder.

'Hide your food,' shrieked Jayne. It was too late, they were attacking, my nightmare coming true, they were nipping Jodie and screeching at Emily. I dared to look up at the sky, it was a wall of seagulls. *Argh!*

Hannah Poulter (11)
Shelf J&I School, Halifax

The Pond Monster

It stood there, small, green, dripping with slime. I couldn't quite see what it was because of the mist in front of it.
Finally it moved forward out of the mist. The creature stood there glaring at me with his bloodshot eyes. 'Why did you push me in the pond?'

Matthew Crabtree (11)
Shelf J&I School, Halifax

The Black Hole

I came to the cave and walked inside. I went deep into the damp hole. Suddenly I heard footsteps echoing down towards me. I hid behind a rock and listened to the sound getting louder and louder! I then heard a voice shouting my name, 'Alex! Alex!' Everything went black.

Daniel Marsden (11)
Shelf J&I School, Halifax

Tiny Tales Yorkshire & Lincolnshire

Doors

There I was coming home on my bike and there was a cottage. I went over to have a look, I knocked on the door but the door was open. I went inside to have a look but the door closed! Then the window shut. I was locked inside!

Joseph Lumb (10)
Shelf J&I School, Halifax

The Deep

Oscar sprinted into the sea in pitch-black, he raced as far as he could. He finally stopped. Just then he saw a figure in the water and again, it was getting closer. It jumped out of the water. It was grey with two fins. Oh, it was a dolphin!

Daniel Wilson (11)
Shelf J&I School, Halifax

No Please No!

It surged towards me, I tried to run but there was not any door that I could escape from. I was trapped.

'No, please no,' I screamed, but that was no use.

Suddenly I stopped pleading and screamed my head off. 'Ow,' I wish I wasn't so scared of injections.

Emily Stott (10)
Sowerby CP School, Thirsk

Pop Goes The Dinosaur

I banged the door and *pop!* a small dinosaur came out. It ran around the room and hid behind a box. But which one? If I didn't find it I would lose my job. I ran and ran and ran. Eventually it jumped into my closed arms and smiled happily.

Jack McLauchlan (10)
Sowerby CP School, Thirsk

Breakfast

The fiery egg mountain was spreading into the forest of bacon. Soon the smooth yellow substance would reach the juice of the fried tomato plantation. Then the sausage barricades would kick in and stop the flow. After that the toast would absorb.
'Don't play with food!' said Mum to me.

Gemma Reynard (10)
Sowerby CP School, Thirsk

Stealing Biscuits

Hiding in my dark corner, I heard the creatures prowling, searching.
Suddenly one of them stopped, catching the smell of my only item.
I darted, trying to find another hiding spot. It was too late, Mum saw me and roared, 'Put back that chocolate biscuit now or there'll be trouble!'

Amy Booth (11)
Sowerby CP School, Thirsk

A Dream

I was scared, really scared! I was lost in a maze. I didn't know where to go.
'Ding, ding, ding!' My alarm clock suddenly rang!
I couldn't believe it had been a dream. I had been so worried!
'Lauren, are you getting up today?' shouted Mum.
'Yes, Mum,' I replied.

Laura Cook (9)
Sowerby CP School, Thirsk

The Sunday Roast War

The boiling brown liquid splashed into the armoury when the soldiers were coming out. *Argh!* The tanks came shooting at the castle. That was brown and wobbly. All of a sudden the cold liquid came pouring down onto the scorched …

Just then Mum shouted, 'Don't play with your Sunday roast!'

Callum Stewart (9)
Sowerby CP School, Thirsk

Tiny Tales Yorkshire & Lincolnshire

Who's There

'Who's there,' I cried and wept over my pillow.
It was too painful. My arms would not reach up.
I bellowed through the rooms.
I heard footsteps. A voice whispered, *'Hii!'* It
was my brother. He jumped into my bed.
My earache had gone.
Was it a dream or …

Rebecca Walker (11)
Sowerby CP School, Thirsk

Information

We hope you have enjoyed reading this book - and that
you will continue to enjoy it in the coming years.
If you like reading and writing, drop us a line or give
us a call and we'll send you a free information pack.
Alternatively visit our website at www.youngwriters.co.uk

Write to:
Young Writers Information,
Remus House,
Coltsfoot Drive,
Peterborough,
PE2 9JX
Tel: (01733) 890066
Email: youngwriters@forwardpress.co.uk